DUNCAN RALSTON IS DEAD

LISA BREANNE

Ebook ISBN: 979-8-9910633-2-6
Paperback ISBN: 979-8-9910633-0-2
Hardcover ISBN: 979-8-9910633-1-9

Cover Artist: Marcelle Silva
Editor: Jyl Glenn
Interior Formatting: Steven Pajak

CONTENTS

**NO AUTHORS WERE HARMED
IN THE WRITING OF THIS BOOK**

ACKNOWLEDGEMENT

"When I was a boy and I would see scary things, my mother would say to me, 'Look for the helpers. You will always find people who are helping.'"

—Fred Rogers

The decision to pursue this dream and write my first book was the scariest thing I've ever done. But from the moment I opened my laptop to start writing, to hitting send on the final product, everywhere I looked, there were helpers. These last two years have challenged me in ways I didn't think I was strong enough to handle, but each time I fell, someone was there to pick me back up and continue on this journey with me. I was never alone.

I can't even begin to list everyone who made this possible; the academy only gave me forty-five seconds.

But to those who held my hand, dried my tears, gave me their invaluable advice, made me laugh, worked long hours to get this ready in time, shared it on their platforms, or checked up on me with words of encouragement and support; you have my eternal gratitude. There's a recurring theme I've heard throughout the horror genre; it talks about believing something into existence. Granted, it's usually used in reference to something nefarious, but in this case, I'm using it to thank each and every one of you for believing my wicked little book into existence. It wouldn't be here without you.

—Lisa Breanne

1 July 2024

FOREWORD

BY DUNCAN RALSTON

This is a true story.

No, it isn't. Of course it isn't. But it *could* be.

After all, people go missing all the time. Many of them even end up dead. Take Julian Sands (of *Warlock*, *Arachnophobia* and *Rose Red*, among many others), for instance. Went hiking one January day in the mountains north of Los Angeles, and never returned. His body wasn't discovered until June. A year later and the cause of death still hasn't been determined, which is said to be typical of cases such as his, due to the state of the remains.

Six months alone in the wild. A broken limb or worse could have made it difficult or impossible to escape. Then exposure. Frigid nights. Snow (yes, it snows in the mountains, even in California, though not frequently). Bears. Coyotes. Vultures. The mind reels.

What I'm saying is, the probability of anyone one of

us dying at any given moment is just as likely as anyone else.

Some of you may now be wondering: How did the dead guy from the title write the foreword to this book?

Well, I'll be honest with you. I'm not dead.

Yet.

But I will be.

Some day. Maybe even soon. (A moment after writing this sentence, I discovered I'd been scratched by the chicken-wire cage out back while picking strawberries, and furiously scrubbed the three-inch-long wound. If I happen to die of lockjaw before this book makes it to print, let this be my obituary.)

But let's start at the beginning, shall we? When Lisa Breanne told me the concept for this book my ego—I mean my *interest*—was immediately piqued. Naturally. Who wouldn't want a book named after them, even if the catalyst of the horror in said book was their own demise?

Some people suggested it was tempting fate. I may have even felt similarly myself—and more so just now, with the tetanus scare—but I bit the bullet, so to speak, and said, *Sure, why not? What's the worst that could happen?*

Fortunately, the worst that could happen isn't likely to be what happens in this book. The catastrophic events that occur after my departure from the literary landscape—as well as the *literal* landscape, unless you count being six feet under said landscape as part of it—are quite harrowing. Not many survive, if any. (I'm not going to spoil it for you. Needless to say, unlike *John Dies at the End*, the *Duncan* of the title is very dead by the end of this one. As dead as Jacob Marley's doornail.)

I realize many of you may know me only from the title of this book, so for you, please allow me to introduce myself (*wink*). I'm an indie/small press author with a couple of cult hit novels, one of which is transgressive horror, though often called extreme horror or splatterpunk. That book is *Woom*, and for the past three years or so I have been under a bit of a spotlight for it. I like to think of it—and a few other modern extreme horror books—as *Baby's First Splatterpunk*. I can't count how many people have told me *Woom* was the first book of its kind that they'd read, and from there they never looked back. It's an odd feeling, a *good* feeling. Especially since when I first started publishing, I expressed to my wife how excited I was that a hundred and fifty people downloaded my "free Canadian eBook" (to quote Dan Harmon, creator of *Community* and *Rick and Morty*), and *some of them might actually read it*! Fast forward to now, where that same book was read and blurbed quite nicely by one of my idols (the late, great Dallas Mayer, aka Jack Ketchum), and there are over thirty-thousand copies of *Woom* out there in the wild, which isn't a mind-blowing statistic for a traditionally published book but virtually unheard of for small press or indie authors.

I suppose I should add, before we continue, the Duncan Ralston of this story is not the real me. There are a great many differences between the fictional me and the flesh-and-blood me. The first, and most important: I don't drive a car. I *can* drive a car—I was pretty good at it, actually—but I let my learner's permit expire almost thirty years ago and haven't driven since. I have no need for a car in the city. Plus, they're expensive, and I'm cheap. I do have my boating license, though, oddly enough.

Still, what happens in this book *is* possible. If you'll indulge me a few more minutes, I'll outline how:

[*Editor's note: the following two paragraphs were so thoroughly spattered with blood as to be indecipherable.*]

And that's how the events of this novel could theoretically come true. *If* I were dead, of course. Which I'm not. At least, as mentioned before, *not yet*.

You see, as part of the agreement I made with Lisa, I took a very rare and slow-acting poison right before I began writing this foreword, whose effects will only come to pass after you've finished reading this foreword. Don't blame her, those four or five of you who may take umbrage with this: it was my idea, not hers. I thought it would be a great marketing ploy for the book, and I wasn't really doing anything noteworthy anyhow. My best work is already behind me. What else am I doing now but resting on my laurels, or perhaps spinning my wheels, desperate to come up with the hotly anticipated follow-up to *Woom*?

That's what my harshest critics might say, anyhow.

To them I say, please be gentle on Lisa and this book. She is a kind and generous soul, and bear in mind, it's her first novel. Until she'd really begun to dig into my life story, she wasn't aware of the kind of monster she was dealing with, the kind of person who'd write a book deserving over twenty-five hundred one-star ratings. (Save your one-star reviews for *Woom*. My wife will need the money.)

Soon, very soon now, that monster will be dead.

Until then, watch the news.

Keep an eye on your social media feeds.

Because when I go, I'm going to take as many of you down with me as I can.

As Annie Wilkes says to Paul Sheldon in *Misery*: *If I die... you die.*

Okay. I'm dying now.

Don't forget me.

Goodbye.

urk

WEEK ONE

Duncan Ralston is Dead.

Or so my Facebook feed says. I lean back in my computer chair and read the headline again and again. One more time for good measure. My mind cannot wrap itself around the words or the repercussions if this is actually true. I have been following the story since he went missing one week ago, and if I wasn't checking my phone every ten minutes while waiting in line for coffee, at the checkout with groceries, or picking up my takeout order for dinner, because who am I kidding? I'm not actually going to cook those groceries, or I was at my desk refreshing my computer screen nonstop while I pretended to watch whatever IDTV show I had playing in the background.

I haven't been able to accomplish any work since two, no, three days after the news broke, but in my defense, neither have a lot of others in my field. However, fortunately and unfortunately, some have taken this opportunity to make themselves seen and heard.

The first post I saw that Duncan had been MIA for twenty-four hours was on a fellow blogger's page. It didn't phase me. *So what? Leave the guy alone; he has more important things to do than sit scrolling social media trolls' uploads,* I thought. A frequent presence in our virtual world of Extreme Horror, it was somewhat unusual for Duncan to be inactive for that amount of time. But with the current circumstances, all eyes were on the moves of every horror author out there in the indie community, and I wasn't initially concerned.

Day two passed without incident. It was the last day of my junior year of college before summer break and has always been my habit; I took the remainder of that day to take a breath, drink some cheap wine, and get absorbed into B-list horror movies while my phone sat on silent so I could decompress.

On day three, I awoke with a start, my alarm blasting the theme music to Tales From The Crypt, alerting me it was time to make myself appear a step above homeless and head to my first class. But I didn't have class. It was officially the first day of break; what I did have, though, was a splitting headache thanks to the bargain wine the night before and morning breath that made me question if I'd gotten a cat and it had shat in my mouth. Attempting to sit up while simultaneously reaching for my phone to check the time caused my head to go from splitting to a full-on cacophony of agony, "Jesus Christ," I whispered as the wine and peanut butter toast I scarfed scarcely more than six hours ago threatened to reappear. I blinked several times, trying to compute the words my eyes were scanning.

Duncan Ralston Car Found Abandoned??? Blood-stains??? Cell Phone and Wallet on Floorboard!!!, the huge headline said, followed by the shocked face and broken heart emojis. This proclamation was posted slightly less than two hours ago by Miranda Kefler in Omaha, Nebraska, and it already had seven thousand reactions and hundreds of comments.

Miranda was a fellow blogger and book reviewer that I had recently started following after she reached out to me about an author I had interviewed. I wouldn't call us friends, but we chat from time to time, mostly through Messenger. I scanned the comments for any clue as to why she would have posted this; where did this information come from? The comments were mostly emojis of hands praying, faces crying, and broken hearts with words like "thoughts and prayers" stated. Then, of course, you have your typical trolls making comments such as "I never really cared for his writing" or "WOOM was a disgusting cash grab by a talentless hack." I generally avoid these comments as they serve no purpose but to advertise the disgusting character of the commenter. However, these trolls occasionally provide some backstory or information regarding statements posing as facts.

I scrolled for about twenty minutes until I finally came across a reply by Candace Cusp that no one else seemed to have seen, as there was no reaction to it. "The car was not abandoned! It was left in a long-term parking garage, and even the police said that what they initially thought was dried blood at first glance, turned out to be congealed BBQ sauce. And nothing was mentioned about a cell phone or wallet; posting a headline such as this spreads unnecessary panic."

I flopped back into my couch cushions and exaggeratedly rubbed my face with both hands, still physically feeling the effects of last night's binge and the ass load of information I had just consumed. I sat there staring at the screen for a few minutes, trying to formulate my thoughts and swallow down the bile that kept teasing the back of my throat. Should I make my own post questioning the validity of the other blogger? No. I'm not one to start unnecessary drama, I do, however, feel like I need a shower and strong coffee before I attempt anything else.

After the initial shock of the scalding water and the bitter hit of the first sip of black coffee, I felt clear-headed and ready to address this morning's claims. As a reviewer and blogger, I make it my business to know everyone else's, especially in the Indie book universe. But I am under no preconceived notions that it actually is, in fact, any of my business. I opted against making a post or commenting on Miranda's and instead decided to reach out to her myself. I was curious where she got her information and why she felt the need to capitalize on it. Shock value, misinformation, and gossip weren't her usual.

I opened messenger, scrolled until I found our last chat session, and typed, "Hey Girl, what's up? Saw your post earlier and it was quite the head-scratcher.... I have questions. Obvs I'm not calling you out just wondering where your info came from. Anyways, hit me up, big story and all."

I closed my laptop and headed into the kitchen in search of sustenance before deciding I didn't want any of the healthy options I purchased when I was a different person. I end up grabbing my keys, phone, and bag and heading out to find something greasy and temporarily satisfying until I step on the scale in the next few days.

Starbucks...no.

Tim Horton's...no.

"Why the fuck did I decide to walk," I mutter to myself.

Cuppa Joe's Café and Bakery... do I feel like being hit on by a bunch of guys with ponytails just to obtain the fatty French toast sausage bagel sandwich the café is famous for?

Begrudgingly no.

Just as my eyes landed on the sign for Gran's Diner and I decided a plate of their

questionable biscuits and gravy, along with a cup of their muddy black coffee, sounded like the perfect cure for my hangover, my phone made its obnoxious ping, alerting me to a new message.

"Hey! Just saw this. My phone has been going mad this morning, mostly bitches being bitches and trolling me for my post.... which btw is at almost 9k reactions!! Guuurl, I haven't gotten this much attention since that fuck face Bruce Seller spread that shit rumor that I blew him on the football field after prom."

Miranda's excessive use of emoji reactions annoyed

me, but I was grateful I at least got a response. I would have preferred it to be after I got my plate of greasy goodness, but whatever.

"Yeah, I see you have caused quite an uproar, where'd you get your info? All I've seen is how he was quote-unquote 'missing'," I replied, hoping I didn't sound as snarky as I was definitely starting to feel towards her after reading how excited she sounded over the response to her post.

"Wellllll," her next message started out, dragging the L longer than necessary to indicate what? Guilt? Attitude? A confession she was about to proclaim? Turned out it was the latter. "You know Mitch, right? The guy who blogs from the comfort of his mother's couch at 34 years old?" Miranda continued.

"Yes" was all I responded, the headache starting to ramp up intensity again.

"So, Mitch apparently lives close to the long-term parking lot his car was found at, and you know how he's always talking about the shit he picks up on his police scanner? Well, I heard he told Marty.... Oh wait, maybe I'm getting them confused. Is it Marty or Mitch that lives in his mom's basement? I can never remember."

Yep, my head is about to explode.

"You had it right the first time; Mitch lives with his mom. I'm not sure who Marty is". I quickly typed as I opened the door to the diner, not willing to stand outside waiting for her responses anymore as I am now in desperate need of the caffeine to hopefully silence the marching band currently performing inside my skull.

"Oh, okay, I do that a lot. There were these two girls in my high school that I constantly got confused, but in my defense, they did look alike and had similar names. I remember this one time when I was running for student body president in like 10th or 11th grade, I don't remember which, but I was up on stage making my first speech, and one of them raised their hand to ask a question about some initiative I had intended on pursuing or something, I called her the wrong name, that was embarrassing lol, probably why I didn't win. But I still think it was the God Damned Bruce guy I mentioned earlier, he was a real fuck face, like I said. I can't believe you don't know who Marty is... I thought everyone knew Marty. Marty is the stoner guy who is constantly commenting on everyone's posts; I'm sure you've seen his comments; he's clearly never sober, but fkn hilarious; I started following him after the altercation he got into with Eve Easterly in one of the book groups."

I had made the mistake of setting my phone down once I was seated and half-assed browsed the menu until the waitress returned with my liquid charcoal, but I could hear that Miranda was clearly on a tangent that I just wasn't prepared to fake interest in at that precise moment.

"Have you decided what you'd like ma'am?" The

waitress asked. Her name tag read Wendi, spelled with an i instead of y. She set my steaming cup of coffee on the table, sloshing it just enough to warrant the use of more than one napkin to wipe up.

"I have. Could I get your biscuits and gravy platter? And I saw you had Bloody Marys, I'll take one of those too, a double, and make it spicy if you can, please."

That came out faster than I had intended, but Wendi with an i just nodded and walked off. I leaned forward and methodically rubbed my temples before picking up my phone to respond to Miranda.

"I remember that, yeah, but Eve intentionally stirs the fkn pot and causes grief for everyone who accidentally crosses her path. I stopped following her a few years ago when she started with her cancel bullshit, and I realized she was talking shit about books she hadn't even read."

Taking a big gulp of the Bloody Mary Wendi had so kindly delivered in the same manner as the coffee, wiping up the table, I continued, avoiding bringing whoever this Marty was back into the conversation.

"So, Mitch is where you heard all those details from?" I asked directly, hoping Miranda would just answer, and I could set my phone down and enjoy my piping hot gravy-slathered day-old biscuits quietly.

"I mean... kinda. So Mitch posted something about it and Marty tagged me in it because we'd been having a discussion about the whole Duncan going missing stuff, mostly theories we'd seen others comment." Miranda responded.

"What do you mean kinda?" I fired right back, not caring about being couth at this point.

"............" popped up.

"Well, if you can keep an itty secret, I maaaay have embellished, just a tad." Miranda sent with a winky face.

"You what???!!!" I shot off. *You have got to be fucking kidding me!* I thought to myself, taking another mouthful of the spicy hangover cure.

"Hey, don't be judgy girl, it's not like I made up the whole thing. They really did find the car and the blood, or what they thought was blood! I basically just reiterated what Mitch had said, only added a smidge to it, and if anything, I was helping becausssseeee have you seen how many people have reacted??? Lots. So really, all I did was bring added attention to wtf is going on, and my followers took a huge jump, and you can't tell me that isn't worth a bit of a fib that hurts no one."

I couldn't believe what I was reading. Fabricating crap is the M.O. of a lot of bloggers, sure. I know some take their favorite words as gospel, but most know it's exaggerated to obtain more likes. I've done it myself a time or two.

"Dude, I get feeding into sensationalism is tempting, and part of what we do is create traction and bring attention to things. But someone is literally missing.

These aren't convention rumors we hint at being truths, but a real-life person we both respect who may or most likely may not be in trouble. And driving up the rumors on something like this could be detrimental, just sayin'. I'm sure he's just taking a hiatus and will be back to posting his jokes and updates any time, but

after the shitstorm that's been circulating through the Indie community and the mud-slinging Eve started. Anything else is just going to cause the wake to continue. I'm not trying to lecture or be a bitch; all I'm doing is pointing out the consequences. Sorry if it came across wrong... and for this novel-length response, lol." To my chagrin, I added a bunch of emojis to hopefully let Miranda know I wasn't angry. I was secretly annoyed and a bit disgusted, but she didn't need to know that.

ping

"Potential consequences." was all Miranda replied.

I paid my bill and left the diner, the borderline migraine having receded to a dull ache just above my eyebrows. As the door swung closed behind me and the warm breeze tousled my unbrushed hair, a wave of exhaustion overtook any thought of doing anything but going home and crawling into the bed I hadn't gotten to enjoy the night before. Starting down the block, I realized just how far I had actually walked earlier on my hunt for food. I had no desire to do that again, so I opted to cross the street and head to the subway station instead. My apartment was only two stops from here, and although I detested the idea of the enclosed space and preferred the smell of car exhaust and hot dog vendors to urine, stale coffee, and b.o., I took a breath and descended the steps to catch the next train.

I closed my eyes and willed the train to go faster. I longed more and more for the comfort of my queen-sized haven. I overheard a conversation that started to take place that pulled me from my half-conscious reverie.

"You know that author worships Satan, right?" The middle-aged woman sitting across the aisle and about five seats down from me said, addressing the gentleman across from her. I glanced in his direction to see if he intended to respond and was curious to know what he was reading to warrant such a comment from a stranger. To my surprise and delight, the man held a copy of WOOM in his hands.

"Excuse me, sir? I don't think you heard me. I know it's none of my business, but I happened to look over and see what you were reading, and I couldn't help but offer you some friendly advice." The woman sounded feeble. The gentleman still hadn't looked up.

"My daughter...." She started saying.

"You're right; it is none of your business." He finally glances up from the pages and briefly states before returning right back to The Lonely Motel.

"Well," she retorted in a huff, clearly offended that

this passenger wasn't more interested in whatever she had to say. "You don't need to be rude to me. I was only suggesting that you may not be aware of the serious accusations against that author, and by reading the filth he puts out in the world, you are not only supporting him but publicly condoning the acts he writes about."

"Publicly condoning? Ma'am, this is a work of fiction. It's just a book. My choice of reading material is frankly none of your concern. Now, if you'll be so kind." His eyes once again returned to the pages, making it clear that this back and forth was officially over.

"It is very much my concern when my teenage daughter, still a child and easily influenced, comes home with smut such as this because some YouTuber person suggested it." Her voice continued to rise and now drew the attention of other passengers besides myself to look in this direction. "If people would consciously make the decision to not fill their minds and hearts with this level of sin and depravity, our children would grow up in a safe and loving world and not feel pressured by their peers to participate in foul behavior. You clearly have no children, or you'd think twice about bringing garbage into your home." There was a smug self-congratulating look on her face as if she personally just saved humanity with her insipid rant. I assumed that would be the end of the conversation.

"Listen, lady, I AM a father, as a matter of fact, and I am on my way to see my son. He is currently a patient at

Saint Josephine Hospital, where he has been for the past several months fighting for his young life. I recently vented the heartache my family is going through to an online book group, and Duncan was kind enough to reach out to me and offer to send some of his books. A gesture that is very much appreciated as I spend countless hours on this subway and sitting beside my son's hospital bed with only my grief. I have nothing but the utmost respect for this author and his kindness and generosity in my time of need. So, if you'll excuse me, but the only filth I see on this train is you."

I couldn't help but smile to myself and think, wahoo, dude, good for you! Even though I kind of wanted to clap; this woman's behavior was the exact thing I was constantly touting against to my followers.

The train slowly came to a stop to let out those getting off at this station. Out of the corner of my eye, I saw the woman rise, preparing to exit. She walked forward briskly with sour indignation plastered on her face. As she was passing her adversary, she nonchalantly reached down and snatched up the man's book from where he had set it right next to him following their altercation and continued out to the platform. I sat there momentarily, stunned at what I had just witnessed.

"Hey!! Hey!! What the hell do you think you're doing, lady? Hey!" the man shouted as he hurriedly gathered his belongings, obviously intent on chasing after her to retrieve his book. Fully awake now, with no more thoughts of crawling into my cozy cocoon, I made the split-second decision to deboard the train behind him, curious to be witness to how this played out. I saw her briskly walking ahead and the man swiftly closing the gap between them, when her arm shot out and deposited the book into the trashcan she was passing by. Only two or three steps behind her, he reached the trashcan a second later and immediately retrieved his belongings into his pocket for a tissue, he began wiping it off.

"What the hell is your fucking problem?" he shouted after her. "Crazy bitch." He said as he inspected the book for any potential damage or lingering debris.

I watched as that last comment clearly got the woman's attention, and she unexpectedly stopped and spun around on her heels and started back towards this poor man who had had enough of her insane antics by the look of exasperation on his face.

"That is the precise language I would expect to receive from someone who clearly has no moral code or foundation. When I see the opportunity to help my community by disposing of garbage, I take it." She spat into the man's face.

The man stood there with a look of shock that he had found himself in this ridiculous situation. They stared each other down, neither one venturing to move so as not to appear as the loser in this battle. Suddenly, the woman snatched the book directly out of his hand, turned, and began shoving it into her purse as she strode away.

"Did you forget to take your crazy pills this morning?" The man questioned as he once again followed after this woman. "That book belongs to me, and you have no right to it; give it back this instant!" His voice was at full authoritative volume now as he reached out to grab hold of her purse.

"I will be disposing of this waste elsewhere." She attempted to pull her purse out of his grip, having no luck as he now had a firm hold of it. "Let go of me," she demanded.

"Just give me my property, and I will." He replied through gritted teeth.

"Let me go... Let me go." She chanted as she twisted, trying to free herself. "Help... help! This man is assaulting me, somebody call the police!" She shouted.

My brain was unable to comprehend the severity of how this had escalated. It felt as if I was watching this entire episode in slow motion. One moment, they were tussling to maintain their grasp on her bag, and the next, he lost his balance, whether from her forceful shove to the chest or losing his footing from the twisting and pulling back and forth. He was stumbling, unable to regain purchase, and the man plummeted off the platform directly in front of the train as it slid into the station.

I closed my eyes and turned my head just before a light spray blanketed me as if clouds had suddenly opened up three levels underground. I knew it wasn't rain. Screams suddenly invaded my ears and it took me a few moments to realize it was my own.

WEEK TWO

I had bathed so many times in the last few days my skin was raw, but no matter how hard I scrubbed or how much soap I used, I still sensed the tacky yet slick feeling of the man's blood on my skin. Realistically, my mind knew that any trace of his DNA was long gone, but the memory, still fresh, caused me to see and feel that his blood remained.

The days passed in a drunken haze of nightmares and take out. Wade Russell, that was the man's name, haunted my dreams. I saw his face whenever I closed my eyes and in my peripheral vision whenever they were open. On day four, I woke up feeling lethargic, my head clearer though since I had run out of alcohol early yesterday afternoon and wasn't quite ready to leave the safety of my cocoon to obtain more. So, I'd spent the day updating my blog and briefly catnapping when exhaustion took over.

I received an immense outpouring of support from my followers, friends, and some family after I shared the experience on the Subway. Normally, I keep my personal life private. That is my strict rule when it comes to running this page and interacting with the authors and fans, but in my stupor, I decided to regale everyone apparently. Luckily, the messages and phone calls were starting to taper off, and when I checked my phone before hopping in the shower, there were only eleven messages and three missed calls. "Good", I said out loud to myself until one message further down the list caught my eye.

"WHY AREN'T YOU ANSWERING YOUR PHONE"?

The first in a string of more boldly written texts from my closest friend, Alex. We'd never actually met in person, but she is who I spoke most often to and confided in. Alex wasn't a blogger like me, just a huge fan of indie horror. We met in a Facebook group a few years ago over our shared love of the genre.

"LADY, I'VE BEEN BLOWING YOU UP!!! WHERE THE BLOODY HELL ARE YOU?"

Alex was from a small town in the UK, a few hours from London. Our chats usually took place either early morning for me, evening for her, or late night for me, early morning for her. The longest ones are my late nights because I am a night owl and often three or four glasses of wine in and relaxed.

"GET ON YOUR DAMN COMPUTER NOW AND CHECK THE NEWS."

The news, being social media, I came to realize over time was the only news Alex actually paid attention to. And there it was. The headline of every post. The topic of every reel. The beginning of the end that I would soon be witness to.

DUNCAN RALSTON IS DEAD

Hours later, eyes sore from reading every comment, watching every uploaded TikTok, Facebook reel and Instagram video, I was still no closer to discovering what had happened. Theories swirled like garbage in a tornado, but was there any validity to any of them? I fucking hoped not.

Suicide seemed to be the consensus. I should say, the

hope of the cancel culture whose sole objective as of late had been to admonish certain horror authors they found offensive; you'd think it would be a waste of their time.

There was one "Influencer", and I use the term very loosely as she is only important in her own mind, Eve Easterly. I had yet to scope out what The Mouth, as I not-so-affectionately refer to her, had to say about all of this. Eve had, unfortunately, been the voice leading the charge against everything and everyone in the horror community that she deemed objectionable.

Before regretfully gliding my mouse to click on the link to watch whatever shit she was guaranteed to expunge, I made the call that alcohol was going to be needed for this as my temper would inevitably flare. I filled my glass and readied myself to watch Eve's latest videos. Cringing, but clicking the most recently uploaded one, I was in no goddamn way prepared or buzzed enough for what came on.

"Well, Gals and Ghouls," (God, I hate when she says that; it's not cute, it's repulsive, she's repulsive) "I am back again tonight to inform those of you that haven't heard, Author E.L. Giles, real name Eric Labrie has been found murdered in a hotel room in Montreal, Canada. Unfortunately, I haven't been able to obtain many details yet, but what I have gathered is that foul play is suspected due to strangulation of some kind. You guys! Isn't this wild? That's two in two days..."

I had to pause the video and take a breath, was she fucking enjoying this?! I detected what appeared to be a hint of a smile on her lips; I suppose it's possible my judgment is clouded by my distaste for her or the alcohol coursing through my body at what feels like a hundred miles an hour.

"First, Duncan Ralston goes missing, and frankly, I'm not surprised. Mr. Ralston has rightfully been under fire for his disinterest in addressing the concerns his readers have expressed about the questionable topics in his books. If you have not been made aware, you can check out my previous uploads to gather the 411 on it all."

Her shit-eating grin was plastered across her face. Fuuuck, really? Trolls, to be more accurate. She was acting as if she wasn't the one stirring the pot, spreading the lies, and fueling the fire. Do I comment? No, but I want to. I need another drink.

I hit play as I stand up and head to the kitchen to pour another glass as a small pit of worry starts spreading in my stomach; hearing her voice is enough; I don't need to see her face.

"Duncan Ralston and many others haaa....."

Eve's words trail off as I step into the kitchen and out of earshot. I emptied the rest of the bottle into my plastic Pantera cup and stared at nothing out my kitchen window. I couldn't help but feel an overwhelming sense of dread; coincidences happen all the time; E.L. could have pissed off a number of people. We really don't know what these authors do in their personal lives.

"I mean, it's wild, am I right? Personally, none of this shocks me. I've had a few comments on my uploads criticizing my cold reaction to events, but you, my faithful fans know that I am not an unfeeling person. Is it cold when you hear of a murderer being beaten to death in prison and internally thinking he got what he deserved? Is it cold when a known child molester is in a fatal car accident, and you think to yourself good riddance? When a scourge of society is removed from this earth, I do not find myself to be cold, but do I care if they are gone? Absolutely not! Personally, I..."

"Personally... personally... I this.... I that.... Blah blah blah," I mutter to myself as I pass through my living room and into my bedroom to grab my laptop charger off my nightstand. She sure thinks highly of herself. As I reach to unplug the cord from the wall, my phone vibrates, alerting me to a new message.

Realizing I hadn't checked or returned messages in several hours, I swiped up to unlock my screen. I've missed several calls and messages in the last few hours. So far, none of them warrant my immediate attention.

A lot of "Have you seen the news about E.L. Giles?"

"Man, wtf is going on, Duncan Ralston is missing and possibly dead, E.L. being murdered! Hope you're holding up okay after what you went through. Seriously, hit me back so I know you're good."

"Where have you been, lady? So much shit going down and you're M.I.A."

"Honey, it's Mom, just checking in on how you're coping; you missed our weekly phone call today; hope you're okay. Dad and I love you."

Shit! I completely spaced what day it was; today has been a blur. Damn to be honest, this week has been a blur, I think to myself as I debate on returning my worried mother's phone call. I take another big sip of my wine and hit the call button as I belly flop across my bed to get comfortable; this is sure to be a lengthy conversation involving gossip about neighbors and members of her retired womens' bowling league she recently joined. Dad's recurring bouts of gout and how he still can't believe the cost of fishing licenses are so damn high since Covid.

"Hey, Mom," I said into the phone in the best sober voice I could muster. My mother has never approved of what she referred to as my "de-stressing activities." Never a drinker herself, minus the occasional glass of champagne to celebrate. She found horror and crime documentaries distasteful, so it didn't leave us with much in common.

"Ohhhh honey," my mom said in her overly concerned voice, with undertones of guilt tripping voice. "I am so happy you called, dear; your father and I have been worried. After your unpleasant incident..."

She has always been able to downplay the most tragic of events, commonly referring to them as "unpleasant circumstances, unfortunate occurrences or sad state of affairs" as she shook her head. After her interjecting a benign, somewhat conciliatory comment, she refused to discuss the issue any further. I remember this one time a neighborhood kid was struck and killed by a drunk driver, and it sparked an outrage in the community, with demands for more stop signs, signals, and speed bumps; the local kids even got involved with council petitions. Oh, but not my mom; she did the same head bowed, eyes fixed on whatever project she was sewing at the time, slight head shake. "Unfortunate accident, that poor family," and that was the end of it.

But this time, I spoke up, "That wasn't an accident, Mom!! That man intentionally got behind the wheel, and his choice led to that kid dying. Something should be done!" My mother stared at me blankly, set down her needles, slowly stood, and crossed the room to where I was standing, clearly attempting to show my frustration at her lack of outrage. She lightly stroked my cheek and smiled, "Honey, let's not focus on unhappy things." Her smile brightened, "Now, why don't you come to the kitchen and help me get dinner going?" And that was that, I realized. My mother and I chose to view the world completely differently.

Some people opt to see the world through rose-colored glasses, while I prefer to live mine in reality through fiction.

"...I hope you haven't closed yourself up entirely. Did you start that little herb garden on your balcony I suggested last time we spoke?"

"No, Mom, to be honest, I haven't done much of anything." *Besides drink*, I thought to myself.

"Oh, well, think about it, gardening is very thera-peutic. Glenda from my bowling league, you remember Glenda, the one who broke her ankle recently?" she stated more than asked, assuming I keep track of the personal lives of her new best friends. "Her doctor told her it would take at least three months to heal and to stay off of it. Well, that was right about the time that her vegetable starts needed to get started, and you know Glenda *(I don't)*, the stubborn woman she is, decided to just plop herself down and spread out on her kitchen table and get them going. And you know what? Gosh darn if her doctor didn't clear her to be back up and moving around after only two. Glenda swears it was the gardening that healed her right up."

"Okay, Mom, I'll think about it. How's dad?"

"Oh, he's in a huff; Todd was supposed to help him rearrange the garage and storage shed this weekend, but you know your uncle, something always comes up..."

I let her continue talking without commenting, zoning out while her rambling slowly faded into the background, and I let my eyes start to close, feeling suddenly very drowsy. I don't know how long I laid in the land between being aware of my surroundings and on a sunny beach sipping cocktails with Chris Hemsworth when my eyes abruptly popped open.

"What did you just say, Mom?"

"Um, which part? The score of last night's game your father lost money on. You know I repeatedly tell him that that money would be better spent tithing to the church, but…"

"Mom!! Mom!! No, before that. What did you say about the author killed in Montreal?"

"Oh! Just a clip I saw on a news channel on Facebook, such a sad state the world has become when one isn't even safe at a nice upscale establishment such as that hotel. They showed a brief clip of the body being wheeled out on some sort of gurney. Luckily it was covered, but my heavens, viewers don't need to be subjected to that, it's quite distasteful if you ask me."

"Okay, Mom, listen, I'm glad we talked; give my love to Dad."

"Okay, sweetie, glad to hear you're holding up. We love you and hope you can come home for a visit soon."

I felt a brief twinge of guilt as I hung up after not participating in our conversation. But I needed to see what she was talking about. After grabbing my laptop from the living room, within minutes, I was deep into various news reports discussing the discovery of a local author found deceased in his hotel room. My mom was right; there were several video clips and photos taken of E.L. being wheeled out on a cot and loaded into the back of a nondescript van. Unfortunately, there wasn't much information regarding the circumstances surrounding his death, so I jumped back over to social media in hopes someone had found out something.

Theories were like a swarm of flies congregating around a huge pile of shit on every booktoker's, blogger's, indie youtuber's, and every Facebook page. A lot shared their love of E.L. Giles' books, or experiences they had meeting him at conventions and interacting with him through social media, and sending prayers to his family. It appeared that foul play was the consensus, but nothing I searched gave any indication other than most believing it was due to some form of strangulation.

I laid my head on my right arm and continued to scroll through the comments; I couldn't believe some of the hateful things being said.

"Anyone who can write the things these guys do is guaranteed to be into some crazy shit and probably had it coming."

"I'm not surprised something like this happened."

"Have you read some of his stuff? You know he wasn't mentally well. Wouldn't be surprised if he did it to himself."

"Does anyone actually care?"

"Deserved!"

"Good on whoever took the trash out."

"Good riddance, it's time for these 'Authors' to go!"

As my eyes closed, overcome with alcohol and exhaustion, I thought to myself,

I wonder what Matt Shaw thinks of all this?

Eric struggled to get the keycard into the hotel room doors mechanism while trying not to drop his luggage, letting out a few expletives as his shoulder bag slid down his arm and onto the floor. He much preferred to be at home, as opposed to dealing with the hassle of packing, traveling and the busy city full of germ-laden pedestrians and street vendors, however, he did look forward to these brief work conferences throughout the year. These two-to-three-day getaways allowed him a chance to breathe and relax without the constant hustle of family life with his wife and kids.

Having baby number three had not been his idea; in fact, it had caused a great amount of stress and contention in his marriage ever since his wife broached the idea two years ago. Eric had fallen into a mundane, comfortable existence of routine, work, sports practices, dinner with wife and kids, weekends spent puttering around the house or attending one of his kid's games, and the occasional date night thrown in. Life was simple. But since his daughter was born and eight weeks premature, life has been turned upside down. He rarely got time to himself, and his wife was constantly on his case to help out more around the house and with the baby. This seminar was a welcome escape from a life he wasn't adapting to.

Setting his bags down on the bed and his suitcase leaned up against the TV stand, he surveyed the room. His company did alright this trip, nice place, appeared clean, no lingering cigarette odor or fresh vacuum marks on the carpet. *This'll do*, he thinks as he tucks his private bag deep inside the closet to be taken out at a later time. Grabbing his suitcase to pull out some slacks and a button-up to change into before heading down for the first of several seminars he was to attend over the next few days, he noticed a pretty significant tear in the cushion of the cuck chair adjacent to the king-sized bed he'd be enjoying all to himself that night.

Not ignorant of the activities that take place in hotel rooms, Eric just preferred there to be no evidence of it. He felt that tear in the fabric of what he assumed was a frequently used piece of furniture based on condition, boring a hole in the back of his head. How was he ever supposed to relax and get into the right mood later for what he had planned with the mental image staring back at him.

Glancing at his watch, he realized he didn't have time to wait for someone to come replace the chair or, at minimum, swap out the cushion, but decided to call the front desk anyhow and inform them of the need for correction.

"Front Desk."

"Hi, yes, um, this is Eric Labrie in room 721. I checked in just a bit ago; I'm here for the Tribeca Conference."

"Yes, Mr. Labrie, how can I help you?"

"Uh, well, there's a tear in the cloth on the chair in my room."

Eric registered how lame he sounded just then, complaining to the twenty-something girl at the front desk about a tear. He could practically feel her eyes rolling over the phone.

"A tear?"

"Well, yes, the ahem... chair... that sits angled towards the bed, the fabric is torn, and I was wondering if there's any way maybe maintenance could remove it or replace it." The other end sat silent for a few moments, and Eric could feel his cheeks reddening in embarrassment for asking.

"You want us to remove the chair in your room because of a slit in the cushions fabric?"

"Yes, please."

"Okay Mr. Labrie, I'll send someone up as soon as I can to tend to your request. Do we have permission to enter your room if you're not in it?"

"Um..." Eric hesitated for a moment, thinking of his private bag he had stowed away in the closet. "Sure, yeah, that's fine. I need to head down to the conference room shortly, so yeah, I won't be here. I appreciate you seeing to this little issue for me."

"Will there be anything else, Mr. Labrie?"

Eric returned to his room and immediately noticed the chair still sitting in the same spot, appearing untouched. Frustration arose in his chest as he made his way further into the room, irritation continuing to build that his relaxing night was now ruined by some innocuous furnishing.

On further inspection, though, he saw that the tear was no longer snaking its way down the cushion, in fact, it looked as if there hadn't been one there at all.

Lifting the cushion up to inspect if it had just been flipped over, a lazy solution in his mind for such an upscale establishment, he saw that that was not the case. Tension immediately released inside him; he was suddenly giddy in anticipation of the night ahead.

Unbuttoning his shirt; he walked over to grab the private bag he had hidden in the closet earlier. In his excitement, he failed to notice the tube of industrial-strength fabric adhesive incidentally left on the night-stand by the flustered housekeeper several hours prior. He removed the bag and placed it on the end of the bed. Eric took his time withdrawing the contents, savoring the feel of each item in his grasp.

Plastic grocery bag from Le Beau Marche'.

A roll of standard masking tape.

Black satin eye mask.

Tube of lube.

And a silk scarf.

Eric opened his laptop and navigated to a secured folder he had set up after his kids had reached a certain age where they got into things. He continued to scroll until he found his favorite track, opened the folder, and had his mouse over the play button.

This little compulsion was Eric's only outlet; he never involved anyone else; hell, his wife didn't even know about it. It helped him; it gave him release and it was a thing all his own.

As he turned out the lights and only left the drapes open for illumination, he began to undress, tucked a towel under the door to muffle any noise, and got comfortable on the bed. Before restraining his left hand to the bedpost with the silk scarf, he placed the eye mask over his eyes and the plastic bag over his head, feeling his oxygen supply restricted, which brought a small smile to his face. He felt his way over the comforter to find the tube of lube and placed it on the nightstand before he hit play and proceeded to secure the masking tape to keep the bag in place for a few minutes until he ripped it off. The cold sensation of the lube hitting his genitals felt like nirvana. The slow, soft moaning coming from his laptop steadily increased in intensity, and each gasp set him on fire. The lube felt stickier than he remembered.

"I did not drink too much!! You're the embarrassment, you ass!!"

Eric heard shouting right outside his hotel room, breaking his euphoria; he lay still, hoping this couple, praying this couple, couldn't hear the sounds emanating through his door. If their words were muffled to his ears, the sounds of gratification coming from his room, in theory, should be the same.

Hand firmly grasping his prick, he continued unmoving and just listening. While he was wishing away this intrusive, intoxicated couple, a few additional seconds lapsed, and his breath became more labored, and sweat started to pool at the base of his neck inside the bag. He finally heard the couple retreat down the hallway, still in a heated debate over alcohol consumption.

No longer in the mood to continue with this self-indulgence, Eric decided to call it a night when he registered he could no longer remove his hand from himself without the excruciating pain of the flesh tearing on his penis.

"Jesus Christ!! What the fuck!!" He cried out as he could feel the blood start to trickle down his thigh.

Anxiety coursed through him like wildfire. He once

again attempted to remove his hand from his now shrunken cock, only causing a louder cry of agony and more blood to flow.

I don't understand...

I can't breathe....

Eric knew he had only a few seconds left before running out of oxygen; the blackness already invading his peripheral vision. If I can rip the scarf, he suddenly realized, but more blood came with the strain it took to try and break his tether.

"Come back," he whispered to the drunk couple as the darkness closed in around him.

Body Discovered Near River

Rescue Crews along the Humber River, close to Highway 17 recovered the body of an unidentified male early Tuesday morning. The discovery was made by Mrs. Rossi, a lifelong resident of Toronto when she had taken her grandson to play at the river near Nort

Johnson District Park. Mrs. Rossi immediately called it in, and crews have been on the scene since 0900. The Toronto Police Service has released a preliminary report stating that the deceased is a white male, ranging from 35-50 years of age, and approximately 6ft. No identification was present at the scene. Although no immediate findings indicate foul play, at this point in the investigation, it has not been ruled out. The decedent was transported to the Chief Coroner and will remain in their care pending autopsy results. Nort Johnson District Park is currently cordoned off while police continue their search of the surrounding area; although regrettable, officials are grateful for the public's understanding and hope to finish up and reopen the park before long.

Come Thursday, the Toronto Police Service station was overrun. With what had initially been concerned citizens intermingled with some fans asking for updates on the identity of John Doe found in the river, to full-on picketing and what appeared to be rioting. Signs reading everything from:

"Roses are red, WOOM is incredible, don't blame Duncan because you're unbearable."

"That's NOT what a WOOM is for!"

"I've made a lot of mistakes in life, but I've never canceled Duncan Ralston."

"Traffic cones are NOT meant for THAT!"

"It's no PUZZLE who's behind his disappearance."

"I'm here for the BLOODBATH."

"Epstein DIDN'T kill himself and neither did Duncan."

"REAL Midwives against Duncan Ralston."

According to the article and accompanying the video clips, several windows had been shattered and thousands of dollars in damage was done to the Tim Hortons near the station. A fight broke out, and both parties involved participated in the picketing, but it is unclear who threw the first of many accusations that brought the individuals to blows. The altercation quickly escalated as more people joined in the fray. Officers had been called, but due to the chaotic scene that was taking place back at the station, it took them extra time to respond, resulting in excessive destruction and injuries. This episode in Toronto went viral, and not just in the Indie Horror community, news stations and webpages were also sharing it. Eve Easterly and many other Booktokers' pages were flooded with new followers eager to share their theories and opinions. The drama was a draw to those who felt themselves entitled. My blog sat untouched.

By Friday, I was out of groceries, wine, laundry detergent, and basically every other hygienic necessity. It was time I sucked it up and left the safety of my apartment, and joined the land of the living again. Regretfully sober and with a pounding headache, I slid my jacket on, grabbed my earbuds, and ventured out. Not three steps into my descent down the stairs toward the exit of my building, I heard my name being called from a few flights above me.

"Hey, wait up, I'll walk down with you."

I let out an inaudible sigh and stopped on the third step. Don't get me wrong, Deven is a sweet guy, but he can be a bit much with his conspiracy theories and inability to take a hint that I'm trying to end the conversation. Think Louis Tully, Sigourney Weaver's neighbor in Ghostbusters, that's my neighbor Deven.

"Thanks for waiting!" He says breathlessly. "I'd been debating on stopping by to check on you, but my mom said that after traumatic events, it's best to just give people space unless they come to you."

Deven is a momma's boy through and through. I don't think we've had a single conversation where he hasn't brought her up at least three or four times. Before giving me a chance to respond, he says, "Did you get the lasagna I left at your door? I didn't know if you heard my knock over the music you were listening to."

"Yes, I did. Thank..." but before I could finish thanking him, he nervously cut me off.

"Oh, I didn't make it, my mom did," Deven replied as he adjusted his glasses to avoid eye contact.

I smiled and gestured down the remaining stairs. "Shall we?" I asked, with a hint of can we hurry this the fuck up, that he didn't catch onto.

We chatted a bit over the next fifteen minutes, finally parting ways as I continued ahead, and he went into the electronics store. I grabbed my phone out of my pocket with one hand as I popped in my earbuds with the other and navigated to the open chat that Amateur-BookPirate was currently hosting on Facebook, figuring I could listen in as I shopped. She isn't one of my favorite influencers, not by a long shot, as I fully believe the only thing she actually reads is the bullshit gossip, then proceeds to regurgitate and exaggerate it to gain followers. Unfortunately, it has worked, especially when she goes live, and opens it up for others to join in. The spectacle that ensues is, I admit, entertaining some-times. But her overall "opinion" on a lot of the authors I love pisses me the fuck off.

".... I can understand the point you're trying to make, Mariah425, but unfortunately, he hasn't ever denied the accusations. I know if it was me that was being questioned by my readers over topics in my books, I would take the time to address their concerns instead of just saying, well, you can't please everyone, and leaving it at that."

I entered the grocery store, grabbed a handheld basket, and headed straight for the wine aisle as I heard AmateurBookPirate announce she was going to invite a viewer onto the live chat.

"I appreciate those of you joining me today to discuss the ongoing turmoil in the horror community, whether you like or dislike an author is your choice, but I think we can all agree that more and more lines are being blurred or just blatantly crossed on what is and is not okay to write about..."

No, no, we do not fucking agree. It is fiction, you daft cow.

"Okay, I'm inviting Author R.M. Moore to join this live. Welcome, R.M.! I appreciate you being willing to talk with me and discuss..."

I tuned out their exchange as I shopped the different types of wine, deciding if the coming days would be more Cabernet or Pinot Grigio. Having not decided on what to buy food-wise yet, I grabbed two bottles of each; better to have it and not need it than need it and not have it, I reasoned with myself.

~LAUNDRY DETERGENT
~TOILET PAPER
~DEODORANT
~PADS AND TAMPONS
~TOOTHPASTE, AND I SHOULD
PROBABLY GRAB A NEW TOOTHBRUSH
WHILE I'M AT IT.
~BREAD
~BAGGED SALADS THAT I CAN FORGET
ABOUT AND LEAVE IN THE FRIDGE DOOR
TO TURN BROWN AND MUSHY...

"Again, thank you to R.M. Moore. I have time to invite one more of you watching to join me. Hmmm...... Give me just a second. I sent the invite to join the live feed, and it should only take just another moment."

~BANANAS
~CANTALOUPE
~AVOCADOS
~CHERRY TOMATOES
~COTTAGE CHEESE

"Welcome to the chat.... Um, let me see, Matt Lutton."

"It's pronounced Luh-Ton, like glutton, not futon." He responded with a definite ire of irritation to his voice. "I'm the author of 10 Drink Minimum and Candy Dish. I thought you might be interested in hearing an opposing perspective, or at least your viewers would..... I...."

"Wait, wait, wait..... who are you?" She cut him off.

"Matthew, Matt, Lutton.... I wrote..."

"Okay, hold on, your name is Matthew Matt?" She said with a slight condescending chuckle.

"No, I.....um..... I publish under Matthew, but I go by Matt."

You could tell she caught him off guard; he was flustered. "I was going to say that you're only discussing viewpoints that mirror your own and are speculative. You are slandering and condemning those in the community solely on the subject matter of their books and not who they are as people."

I like this guy, even though he comes across as a bit dim, I thought to myself as I headed in the right direction to snag my last item. I needed chocolate, preferably dark, before checking out. I was already regretting the number of things I had grabbed, that I was now going to have to lug home.

"Well, Matthew Matt Lutton, I've never heard of you; how about you guys?...No? Okay, I appreciate you weighing in, but unfortunately, that's about all the time we have left on this live." He tried to interject something I didn't catch before she booted him off. Wow! What a bitch!

"Oh! Before I let you all go, I want to thank all of you again for jumping on and listening to me ramble and for contributing your thoughts. A special thank you to R.M. Moore for providing insight into writing horror with heart and understanding where we as a community are coming from regarding feeling violated by certain authors' misogyny towards women."

"Violated, my ass!" I said and rolled my eyes as I joined the line for checkout, not realizing I said it out loud until the lady in front of me turned around and scowled.

"But an especially big shout out to whoever sent me these amazing-looking cupcakes!!" She squealed like a child. *Oh lord*, I thought as I unloaded my groceries onto the belt. "There was a note attached that said, you deserve this, no name though... sad. I wish I could personally thank you. Just knowing that you appreciate me and that maybe I'm making a difference is reward enough. But in case you're watching..."

I could hear her opening the package as I continued

to empty my basket. Then she proceeded to take what I assumed was a big bite of cupcake and attempted to say "oh my god, soooo yummy." Again, rolling my eyes, no one wants to hear or see you gorging yourself, lady, yuck. The sound of her licking her lips and making those little moaning noises was turning my stomach. I wish I could crack you open now. I thought about the bottles of wine I had started to place on the conveyor.

"Wow! That was so good. Anyway, pending my work schedule *ahem*, and new

developments *cough*, sorry guys, I have a tickle in my throat or something *cough* *cough*. I plan on *ahem* posting a few Tik Tok (clears throat) review videos in the near *ahem* future *ahem*. God I'm sorry .....*cough* *ahem* *cough* I think.... *ahem* I think ..... I think I might be choking *cough*."

A wine bottle in one hand, I pulled my phone out with the other. I didn't need to listen to her hacking up a hairball. But when I went to exit out of the video, I could tell right away she was, in fact, choking. No, not choking, aspirating. Her skin was covered in hives? Blisters? I couldn't tell. A thick foam-type substance oozed through her now blue-gray lips as the blood vessels in her eyes began to burst. Jesus fucking Christ, what was happening to her?! Wasn't anybody home? Could no one hear her thrashing?

"Ma'am, did you still want that bottle of wine?"

I heard the cashier, but I couldn't respond. I couldn't

look away. I couldn't make myself do anything but watch this girl writhe in agony, suffocating on her own bile.

"Ma'am, were you intending to purchase that?" the young clerk repeated.

"Miss, are you alright?" A soft male voice behind me asked.

Her shallow breaths came in intermittent gasps until none came at all, her blood-red gaze vacant and lifeless. I looked up and locked eyes with the checker as tears began cascading down my face. That moment, trapped in limbo; the sound of the wine bottle shattering was the only noise to break through.

I am a great girlfriend, I love being in a relationship, I love going out on dates and fixing myself up to make my boyfriend's friends jealous. I love the feeling I get from preparing a meal they love, screaming along with them at the TV during sports games, cuddling up on the couch to watch their favorite action flick, or pretending to be scared during a horror one. I also consider myself a fairly decent lay; I'm adventurous and make all the right noises, say all the right things, and I'm willing to try "new things I've never done before." Scratch that; I'm not a great girlfriend; I'm a fucking excellent one… until things get hard. I've never been good at empathy.

Not being someone who enjoys the awkward aftermath of one-night stands or no-strings-attached hookups, I have chosen to remain single for the time being.

I did have one threesome recently, well, a two-and-a-halfsome, I'm 5 '2, and they were both college basketball players. But that's the extent of my prowess these days.

What I don't do is wake up in strange beds to the smell of coffee and the awful cacophony of Nickelback coming from the other room. And I certainly don't feel the need to make excuses about why I am leaving in a rush and I don't let myself get guilted into dinner later.

Yet here I am, about to knock on the door to Deven's apartment because I drank too much the night before. God, I hope he'll just let me explain that I was in a bad place after having just watched a woman choke to death, and I needed a comforting distraction, my resolve coming to an immediate halt however, when his mother answered the door.

"Oh! Mrs. VanKirk. I was expecting Deven." I said with a nervous chuckle while internally screaming *fuuuck.*

"Come in, come in, dear. I hope you don't mind me

joining your dinner date. I swung by earlier to drop off a few things, and Deven informed me of your plans."

"Um, well, it isn't really a da…"

"Let me just say that I am absolutely just tickled my boy finally got his nerve up. He's been smitten since you moved in, don't cha know." She said with a wink.

"Mom!" Deven chastised, coming around the corner from the kitchen.

"I'm so glad you could come," he said as he lightly put his arm around me and kissed my hairline. What the fuck is this? Does he think we're a couple now? I stood rigid, and he dropped his arm. Mrs. Vankirk smiled ear to ear at us the whole time. I read and watch a lot of horror, but this whole situation is just unsettling. I halfheartedly returned her sentiment, and in my most forced polite voice, I asked if I should return to my apartment for a bottle of wine.

"Gotcha covered." Deven winked at me while pulling out an expensive bottle of red from a grocery bag. "Why don't you ladies take a seat, dinner is almost ready."

"I hear you do something with computers, dear?" She inquired as she chose the chair across from me, leaving the only other available one next to me for Deven.

"Sorry, what?… Oh, um, yeah, kind of. I have a blog I run. It's like an online journal." I muttered, my eyes continuing to drift towards the door.

"Oh, how interesting, what do you journal about?"

"Books mostly. I read a lot."

"Oh lovely, I used to so enjoy cozying up with a good Danielle Steele or Debbie Macomber when my eyesight was better. Do you ever write about them?"

"I haven't," I said, hoping she wasn't picking up on my urge to bolt the hell out of there. One thing I despise more than meeting parents is small talk. "I primarily read horror." I stated.

"Oh goodness." her eyes got wide. I could tell I just made her uncomfortable; I will never understand the assumptions people make. I felt the heat in the pit of my stomach start to churn, mentally preparing myself to go to bat for my preferences.

I went to respond when Deven came out carrying a lasagna.

"Grub's up," he said with a big grin. I found myself starting to relax as he dished up his mom and me, pouring us both a generous amount of wine. Maybe I could just enjoy this evening and stop overthinking it. I like Deven's company well enough; he's got a real geeky quality to his personality, not my type at all, but the awkwardness is slightly charming.

"I read a few Stephen King stories years ago. Not my cup of tea; I think there's enough scary things going on in the real world, like the library that group set on fire earlier today. There were innocent people inside, can you imag..."

That got my attention. "What library?" I practically shouted.

"Oh, well dear, I don't recall the name of it right off hand. Somewhere up north." She stammered, taken by surprise by my outburst.

"Do you remember anything else? Name of the town? What kind of group?" I knew I was frantically grilling this poor woman, but I had this ick feeling making its way throughout my body.

"Um, I think it was Grove something, Meadow Grove may…"

"Mile Grove? Was the town called Mile Grove? Does that sound familiar? Was it half brick with a large over-hang at the front?" I felt the bile in the back of my throat and the flush in my cheeks. I appeared crazy to these people I barely knew, but I had a gut feeling this wasn't just some random arson; this was only the beginning.

Back at my apartment, I immediately grabbed my laptop, searching for any news article, interview, or police report I could find regarding this fire. My heart sank as soon as I read the headline: Mile Grove Public Library Set Ablaze, Total Loss Says Fire Chief. I read the write up, which didn't give much insight into any details; I was able to ascertain that a small group of individuals showed up holding signs and encouraging patrons not to support this facility. Other sites were more helpful, luckily, and some news crews were able to grab a couple of interviews from witnesses. Mile Grove Library is well known for supporting independent authors; their horror selection was quite impressive. Often hosting signings and seminars and advertising events on their billboards etc. This was truly fucking heartbreaking.

The choking death of AmateurBookPirate the day prior had spurred a miasma of hate-fueled accusations. A local group of her followers and an array of others who also assumed it was someone in the horror community got together to vocalize their beliefs by protesting the library's support of indie horror. It got out of hand. Fights broke out, police were called, but no one was able to determine who started the fire as of yet. Interviews were still ongoing.

Looking through the pictures and video clips, I was shocked to see Ben Young amongst the crowd. I personally haven't had much interaction with the author, but he always came across as docile and quiet, one of those guys who blend in wherever he is. Was he there? He had one of those I-don't-remember-him kind of personalities. Wait! Is he siding with the protesters?! You've got to be fucking shitting me! Why is he standing with them? I hit play on the recording a local news station had uploaded; it was hard to hear what the reporter was saying with the cacophony in the background, but the few words I was able to catch felt like a punch to the gut.

"Chauvinist."

"Rapist."

"Sicko."

"Groomer."

"Misogynist."

"Pedophile."

It's one thing to see these comments on social media but another entirely to hear them coming out of the mouths of real people, not that it's not real people posting these things, but it's easier to brush it off when you don't see the loathing in their eyes.

"Sir… sir? Could we have a minute?" The reporter was trying to get the attention of someone in the crowd.

"Hi, thanks for taking a moment to speak with us. Can you tell us what's going on here?" The gentleman she pulled over looked like a deer in the headlights.

"Whelllll, I just showed up not too long ago to return these here books I borrowed, and this here angry group wouldn't let me in. Seemin' they mad over some authors or some such, but I ain't know nothin' about that."

"What made you decide to stick around once you realized entry into the library was blocked?" the reporter questioned.

"That there's my truck over there; I'm blocked in

now that more people saw fit to show up and just park where they wanna. You ain't gonna hear me complainin' none though; you see these here gals in them short skirts, I tell ya's I ain't seen noth..."

"Well, thank you for talking to us; good luck with your truck." The reporter cut him off quickly and gave the camera a wide-eyed good-lord expression that made me chuckle. "Let's see if we can get someone else; hmmm." She said to who I assume was behind the camera. "Ma'am, hi. Would you mind if I asked you a few questions?"

"Sure, sure" the woman responded, "What all you wanna know?"

"What brought you here today? I see you're holding a sign. Am I safe in assuming you are part of the group upset with this facility?"

"You bet your ass I am upset, I been sayin' all along these so-called writers out there spreading this filth need to be put to a stop. Libraries shouldn't be supportin' this junk, ya know, young minds comin' here to learn and see this junk, and it's corruptin' them."

"There appears to be a large crowd..."

"God fearin' crowd." The woman said with adamance. I couldn't help rolling my eyes at that. Your faith has nothing to do with why you're there, lady. *Betcha, if that camera were to pan down, we'd see Live, Laugh, Love plastered on her somewhere*, I thought to myself.

"I'm noticing lots of signs here with some pretty harsh opinions and accusations; what does yours say and why that particular statement?"

"I will not raise my children in Shawdom and Gomorrah." The woman stated proudly.

"Don't you mean Sodom?" The reporter interjected.

"No, Ma'am, that Matt Shaw writes nothin' but trash, encouragin' sin and premarital fornication. I caught my daughter with one of his books, and when I tell you some of the stuff I saw in it, Lord, I was beside myself with worry for her soul."

"Oh, for fuck sake!! If your daughter is going to Hell, it's not for reading a book you self-righteous cow." I chastised my computer monitor before pausing the video, my temper boiling to the surface. To avoid chucking my laptop across the room, I carried it with me to the kitchen to pour myself some wine and change my environment, a tactic my therapist suggested whenever my anxiety got the better of me. Taking a very generous gulp, I clicked the play button on the next video; at first, it just appeared to be surveying the scene. People were carrying their signs, yelling in protest, both sides getting in each other's faces, defending their stance.

I almost navigated to another page when the video captured smoke starting to billow from the east side of the building. Whoever was holding the camera started jogging with the crowd toward it. The closer they got, the worse it was. The entire back side of the building was ablaze. Shouts of "Someone call 911!" and "We need to get everyone out!" mixed with whoops and hollers of excitement. My heart raced as I watched the devastation unfold like a bad B-movie.

A scream erupted, unlike anything I've ever heard, guttural, terrified... the camera swung back and forth, clearly searching for the source, and landed on a woman pointing towards a window engulfed in flames. "Stop fucking moving," I shouted at the cameraman who obviously couldn't hear me, but fuuuuck!! What was she pointing at?! The camera suddenly stopped... and began to zoom towards the window. Is that a...a person?? *Holy shit! Holy shit! No... No... No....!* Behind the glass was what I can only assume was a woman, or what was left of her. Her skin left streaks of melted flesh as she clawed at the window, her hair completely burned off, and remnants of her dress melted to what remained of her body. The blackness of the smoke mixed with the dancing effulgence of the inferno made the whole picture feel like gazing on the portal to hell, being damned for the whole world to see.

Out of camera shot, an object came flying towards the glass, hitting it with just enough force to shatter it. In the same second the oxygen meeting the flame exploded in violent fury. The screen went black.

Mile Grove Local News:

"A fire broke out on the west side of the building to an eruption of cheers from some of the onlookers, Mile Grove Public Library was built in 1964 and has been an ongoing source of entertainment and learning in this community, this is a huge loss of such a beloved institution. We will be updating our social media platforms as more details emerge and witness accounts are verified, despite our efforts, Matt Shaw could not be reached for comment at this time."

INTERLUDE

This was not the plan.

This is a way out.

Where did things go wrong, huh?

When did the world become so ugly?

Back when I started writing, back when WOOM was just a passing idea and not the catalyst on which I built my writing career, if someone had told me I would be sitting on this rock, looking at the same river I had skipped stones across as a child and wondering if I could do it all over, would I change anything? What if instead of attaching myself to my father's stories, I had shown more interest in his fishing, maybe I would be a fisherman right now. Maybe I would be out in the Atlantic at this very moment, wind in my hair, the smell of salt permanently in my nose, a wife and maybe kids anxiously awaiting my return.

Nope, I have come full circle, I am where it all began and contemplating the end. No wife, no kids. Only a cold cup of Tim Hortons shit coffee and a box of Cap'n Crunch cereal to keep me company. Pathetic. And that's definitely not salt I am smelling, it is stale beer and the poor-decision piss of a teenager who thought he would impress his friends by drinking the whole eighteen pack, with the undertones of dirty river water. Fanfuckingtastic. This used to be a nice spot, but now it's a breeding ground for horny boys trying to score with their girls, and kids to defy their parents' rules of no alcohol consumption and illicit substance experimentation.

I chuckled to myself as I realized I sounded like a grumpy old fart. Hell, that's exactly what I am, who am I kidding? Slowly tossing pebbles into the river, watching the ripples morph in the waves, the sound of footsteps crunching down the gravel path towards my location steadily grew with proximity.

"Kinda looks like warped snatches if you turn your head just right." The voice behind me observed.

Without needing to turn around to see who that mouthpiece belonged to, I smirked and replied, "Well, if anyone is the expert on warped snatch, it's you."

"I see you still snack like a ten year old boy." The voice chastised.

"Reminds me of when things were as good as they were ever going to get."

"Well, that's uplifting. Have you considered motivational speaking if this whole writing thing shits out?"

"One nation, under God, indivisible…, yet we are all divided, and God is nowhere to be found," I responded, half-heartedly tossing another stone into the water.

"Again, inspiring. But aren't you Canadian?"

"Semantics."

"You're angry, I get it. It's definitely changed since we first got started. Take a walk with me, mate."

"A walk?"

"Yeah, you got me out here, do you just want to sit and pensively stare at the snatch ripples like some fucking John Denver album cover?"

I stood, "Where to?"

"How the fuck should I know, I'm not from here."

We walked side by side along the river for a few minutes, and I realized I was actually glad he was here. I didn't think he would come; we had never been close friends, I had always thought of him as kind of a dick, but I knew he would understand.

"Did you hear what happened to Gage Greenwood?" he asked, finally breaking the silence.

"Who?"

"Bloke who wrote that Kevin Bacon book. Some bonnie melted his knob off."

"Wait, what?" I asked incredulously.

"Well, not off-off, but enough damage he can't wank one out."

"You're fucking lying."

"I never lie about wanking." He said, winking at me.

"Shit. How did it happen?"

"Supposed fan he met at a signing; guess she didn't like the book." He joked, but I could see the apprehension in his expression. These attacks on horror authors were becoming more and more frequent. We hated to admit it, but we were all scared.

"How did she....um... melt it off?"

"Lye."

"What!!"

"In the condom"

"Fuuuuuck" I sighed, shaking my head in disbelief.

We continued in silence for a while, both replaying in our heads the various hookups throughout our careers and how sideways they could have gone. We ended up back where we started when he finally spoke, "You ready, mate?"

"As ready as I'll ever be."

"Do you have everything you're going to need?" he asked as we got into the car.

"Well, I'm thinking I probably won't be needing the rubbers anymore," I chided.

He rolled his eyes and closed the door.

"What? No comment?" I laughed.

Mile Grove Library was just the first. Hundreds of places across the country have been targeted since, and not just libraries but bookstores as well. This morning on the news, I watched as Bobzbay Books in Bloomington, Illinois, burned to the ground. Liz, the owner, didn't make it out. She was a friend, a confidant, and a huge supporter of the indie horror community. I didn't think I had any tears left after everything I had seen the last few weeks, but this one hurt; this one hit home; this was a personal loss.

I had spoken to Liz frequently over the last several weeks, encouraging her to close the store for a while as the violence was only escalating. Still, she refused, saying now more than ever, it was important to remain a voice of support. I admired her resilience, but in truth, I was scared. Duncan was presumed dead at this point, and that fact only spurred on the cancel cultists. They took credit, and no one came forward, but you could see by their actions that they believed their influence brought on his death in some way, whether by his hand or someone else's. It gave them power. They ran with it, demanding change by any means necessary. If you weren't for them, you were against them.

Eve Easterly was leading the charge from the comfort of her computer chair; she never out-and-out said to perpetrate these protests, but she didn't condemn them either. Often leading her "followers" to people and places she felt needed "changing." She'd recently recorded a video on her YouTube channel where she invited authors to join in and essentially defend their books; it was a witch hunt. I had not watched it yet; the thought of giving her even one more view abhorred me, but curiosity had won over, and I sat down, preparing myself to hit play.

"Welcome, friends," She started out. Her smile reminiscent of the evil faces Charlize Theron's character would glimpse in the movie The Devil's Advocate. It sent chills down my spine.

"I have news!!" She exclaimed triumphantly. "But first, I want to thank each and every one of you; this birthday was better than any I've ever had. The fact that so many people that I've never even met support my cause and are willing to stand up and make a difference is humbling. I'm just a nobody art school dropout...."

"Yeah, so was Hitler," I said out loud with an eye roll.

"Who was Hitler?" came a voice standing over me. Deven put his hand between my shoulder blades and started rubbing small soft circles. We'd been spending a lot more time together recently, I had started posting to my blog again and in turn have received some threatening remarks, so Deven has been keeping a close eye, making sure none of these admonishments are carried out.

"I didn't hear you come in," I smiled up at him.

"You were pretty focused, it looked like. When you didn't answer my couple of knocks, I got worried and tried the door. With the messages you've been getting, it's probably not the best idea to leave it unlocked. I walked right in, and you didn't even notice." He said scrunching that little crease between his eyebrows I've become accustomed to seeing on him.

I wouldn't say we are a couple, but his presence is

growing on me or maybe I just like the comfort of another person to vent to. "Got it." I nodded and smiled.

"So, who's Hitler?" he asked again, eyeing my computer screen briefly as he headed towards my kitchen.

"Eve", at this point Deven was well versed on the situation and my distaste of her. "It's the live she did where she brought in authors to 'discuss' their books."

"Grab your torch and pitchfork," he jokingly exclaimed with a fake scowl, walking back and handing me a glass of wine as he scooched up next to me on the couch and gave me a big cheesy grin I couldn't help but chuckle at.

I forwarded the video a few seconds; I wasn't interested in listening to her self-deprecation while simultaneously kissing her own ass spiel.

"My first guest today is R.M. Moore; most of you are aware he was one of the callers who spoke with AmateurBookPirate during the live where she devastatingly choked to death in front of all her viewers. I'm happy you are willing to speak with us today, Robert. Do you mind if I call you Robert?"

"Sure, yeah, Robert is fine. Thank you for having me, Eve." He seemed apprehensive.

"So, Robert, I'm assuming you probably don't want to discuss the aftermath of AmateurBookPirate's unfortunate accident, whose real name is Cameron Jones for those tuning in, and what your experience was following her passing? There was a lot of speculation on you…"

"Well, I wouldn't say a lot, I…" he was fumbling already, shit.

"The police did show up at your door, correct?" She knew they had; he had been open about it on his social media accounts, but you could see she was intentionally trying to make him uncomfortable.

"Yes, they did, but it was only to interview me to see if I had any insight as to who may…"

"But why would they have come to you? I mean, it wasn't as if you two were friends…"

"No, no, I guess they just… um… because I was considered a witness, maybe. I really don't…"

"Do you think that because of the topics in some of your published works, you were initially considered a suspect?" She continued to cut him, obviously to maintain the upper hand and make him appear nervous and unreliable, which, unfortunately, she was accomplishing.

"Her death was ruled an accident quickly. I don't believe…"

"Yes, severe nut allergy that the neighbor she babysits for was unaware of, yes." Eve wasn't interested in the details of her demise; she clearly had a plan here… what was she trying to do? "I'm not suggesting you would ever have had anything to do with harming her, Robert, only to point out that it was unusual for the police to question you, who had no real prior interaction with her."

"They led me to believe they were gathering witness statements, that is all; at no point was I under any suspicion of being involved. Hell, I live several thousand miles away. I offered to speak to them, I wasn't..."

"You're getting upset, Robert; I apologize. My sole reason for even bringing it up was to show that horror authors such as yourself write about some questionable topics, and it's only natural for others to wonder..."

"I agreed to come on here because I was under the impression we were here to discuss my books and where I get my inspiration, not my culpability based on fictitious stories." He said defensively.

"That's exactly it. You admit some responsibility in other's assumptions..."

"No, no, that is not what I'm sayi..."

"That, in general, there are some subject matters that are just not appropriate and warrant concern. No normal person thinks..." She drug out the word normal for dramatic emphasis and I could hear R.M.'s breath catch. I was expecting him to lash out but luckily, he kept his cool.

"I'm going to refill my wine," I said, jumping up to head to the kitchen. I really didn't need to as I hadn't drunk enough of it yet, but I needed to step away. I don't know why I suddenly felt claustrophobic, my surroundings shrinking by the second. Staring out the window, I could see into the apartment in the neighboring building. A woman was walking around in sweats and an oversized t-shirt, phone up to her ear, while a toddler in nothing but a diaper danced around on the couch, no doubt to some song the cartoon on the TV was playing. I zoned out for a minute until I heard Deven shout out, asking if I was alright.

I sat back down on the couch sans wine, as my head was already feeling heavy, I caught the tail end of what had clearly been a tense few minutes since I'd stepped away.

"Eve, Ms. Easterly. Your pretense to get me on this segment to discuss my novels only to continually berate the genre to hopefully draw attention to yourself is not just ignorant but juvenile. I sincerely hope the rest of your day is as pleasant as you have been." And with that, R.M. left the live. The look of condescension on Eve's face clearly conveyed she didn't give two shits about offending this author; she almost looked triumphant that she had been able to piss him off.

"Hmmm, well, he obviously didn't appreciate the point I was trying to make. Some of these guys get so defensive, it makes you wonder..." She said, intentionally planting that seed of *what are they hiding*.

"Moving on to our next guest, now I admit I'm not familiar with him, but when I posted about having authors on this segment, he responded." Eve stated with a little shrug, "Hopefully, he's not as thin-skinned and open to discussion. Let's welcome Matt Lutton, author of Minimum 10 Drinks and The Candy Dish. Hi Matt, thanks for coming on. Can you hear me?"

"Yes, hi, I can hear you just fine. It's Lutton. Like button, not like futon."

"Excuse me, I misprono…"

"The L-U is a luh sound, not a loo sound. You get it. Luh-Ton."

"Oh, here we go again with this chucklehead, this guy's got the personality of a Ficus." I said with an eye roll. Deven chuckled and leaned back onto the couch.

"I kinda like him. He has an awkward, obnoxious Ross Geller quality to him."

Rolling my eyes again. "Don't think you can charm me with your Friends knowledge." I smiled while giving him a playful shove.

"So Matt, what has your experience, if any, been in regard to readers' angst against topics that should not be used for entertainment purposes, such as S.A., rape, sodomy, pedophilia, grooming, violence towards women, and women being portrayed as the weaker sex?"

"The way I look at it is, if it makes you uncomfortable, it's horror. No one is forcing you to read it; it is your choice. If a book or anything for that matter isn't for you, move on." He responded.

"So, what you're saying is that women shouldn't get a say in how we are being portrayed or mistreated in literature? Wow, that's a very misogynistic stance to take."

"That is not what I said, ma'am, this is fiction, this is…"

"Fiction that bleeds into real life." She interjected, "It's these stories being written that are perpetrating the mistreatment of women, basically giving men a pass to use and abuse us."

"That is not at all what is going on, for example; in my book, which is 10 Drink Minimum, by the way…"

"Like anyone cares." She retorted. "These victims are women who…"

"THESE VICTIMS ARE NOT REAL!" He shouted. "The problem is you people…"

"You people huh? We've sunk to being pigeonholed into second class citizens in your eyes because we've decided enough is enough?" She was getting a sick satisfaction in spinning his explanation to fit her narrative, you could see the delight in her eyes, hear it in her tone.

My computer pinged at that moment, letting me know its battery was running low. *Maybe that's a good thing,* I thought; I don't know how much more of this I can watch. I don't even like the guy, but I felt sorry for him. He was right and getting slaughtered for it.

"Take Matt Shaw for example, he's a well-known, respected author with over two hundred books published and thousands sold…"

"Matt Shaw is a menace!! He repeatedly has shown his disregard towards women but continues to get praised by this community, further proving the blatant hierarchy in indie horror. It's bullshit!" She was riled up, mentioning Shaw had gotten to her. They had had a verbal altercation in the past, and she evidently wasn't over it. Her discomfort tickled me in a way; she had been grossly out of line in her attack, and the readers had seen right through it.

The ping alerted me again, another warning that the battery was dangerously low, and my laptop would soon power down, followed by a notification that someone had sent me a private message.

Eve continued, her voice increasing in pitch and frustration, "Since this entire ordeal began, his support is unwavering. Where is he, huh? Where is the son of a bitch? Why hasn't he spoken out in support of his missing associate? BECAUSE HE DOESN'T GIVE A SHIT, THAT'S WHY!!! Open your eyes to this!! It's over!! For all of you!!" She was breathing heavily now, her face a contorted miasma of anger and hatred.

The silence that followed was palpable, I realized I was holding my breath, but I couldn't release it. The exhalation stuck, as if waiting for something. She lifted her head, appearing to make eye contact with those of us watching. The smile that slowly spread on her lips forged in ice. My screen went black, but I could still hear her.

She took a calm, even breath and with a quiet reserved chuckle said, "You have no idea what's coming, you stand for nothing... and you will fall, and as it comes, your beloved author... cannot be reached for comment."

<h1 style="text-align:right">WEEK SEVEN</h1>

Don't think for one minute you can just fly under the radar. We see you. We follow you. Your words carry weight, a burden we will be happy to relieve you of if you keep running your mouth. Best be watching your back BITCH!

This wasn't the first time I'd been threatened, it was the first one that implied harm though.

See me how?

Followed in what capacity?

What did they mean by my words carrying weight?

Deven took it very seriously, he immediately called the police. Like I said prior to him making the call, with the message coming from a fake Facebook account, there was likely nothing they could do. And according to them, there wasn't. There was no end to the list of people it could possibly be, my blog alone had somewhere around 18,000 followers, and my social media had over 22,000 across all platforms. It could be any one of them. Or none of them at all.

I was hypersensitive to my surroundings for the first several days after reading it. I attempted to have a nonchalant attitude towards threats made via social media, but this one felt different, more foreboding. I could sense the intent in their words. Deven must have picked up on my trepidation because he hadn't left my side, insisting it was no big deal and he could just work from home for the time being.

When no more messages or friend requests from phony accounts came, even after I posted a lengthy blog entry regarding trolling, I felt confident it was nothing more than an occupational hazard. I chalked it up to likely being someone I had recently been in a heated comment debate with regarding Ben Young's stance on the actions of the cancel cult. Ben and I used to be friends, well at least cordial with one another in group pages and chats but lately, I have found his views and support of those who wish to nullify the horror genre alarming. I have tried reaching out on several occasions to question his motivation as a blog topic, which I would like to understand before writing him off completely. Unfortunately, he hasn't responded, only laugh-reacted to some of my comments on his posts. Dick.

"Are you almost ready?" Deven asked, peeking his head around the bedroom door frame. I wasn't. I had only made it as far as putting on a bra and underwear after the shower. Towel still wrapped around my head, I sat on my bed scrolling various media outlets. "Did you still want to go?" He asked when I didn't respond.

"Yes, sorry. I got lost in thought for a bit, I'll finish getting ready now." I said, smiling at him to ease the worry I could see on his face. "I'm okay, really. Just getting distracted is all. I've been looking forward to this convention forever, looks like it might be the only opportunity I can get to talk to Ben Young." I chuckled and rolled my eyes. I really was okay and was actually excited about attending SplatterCon. The tickets had sold out fast, and I had been lucky to score some.

"Jesus Christ, would you look at this line to get in? You all sure take your love of horror seriously, some of these costumes are wild." Deven exclaimed, his eyes huge as we entered the convention center. I couldn't help grinning while I watched him take it all in. I wove my arm through his and guided him over to a blown-up map of the event. Ben's panel was early, and I wanted to make sure I knew where I was going so I didn't miss it.

We went and snagged a table at the little coffee bar; I desperately needed caffeine and a chance to go over my questions for Ben. "Will you grab me a..."

"Quad shot americano over ice, extra ice, with a splash of cream." He finished my question with a wink and a smile as he headed up to the counter. I watched him for a second, I haven't been in a relationship in so long, is that what this was? It seemed "relationshippy" minus the awkward getting-to-know-you phase like we jumped right into 6 months in. We were sleeping together but it felt more like a comfort than the obligatory frantic fucking that came with every new partner. I wonder if he feels the same way. Maybe we should talk... later. I've got to focus. I only had about 10 questions written down, but my main objective was to corner him into explaining himself. I was pissed and I know a lot of others in the community were as well.

It took you several years and multiple drafts to complete Stuck. Did the finished novel end up being what you originally set out for it to be?

I know a lot of authors get asked what their inspira-

tions are, but I'd like to know what were some of your negative influences that pushed you to write?

You just released your second novel, and like your debut, it became an instant hit. What would you say to another newer author who hasn't found the immediate success you did and feels like quitting?

Typical interview questions. I felt like jumping down his throat, but I knew using that approach right out of the gate probably wouldn't garner the answers I was looking for. I was hoping starting with the mundane would catch him off guard.

"In light of recent controversy in the indie horror community, I'd like to ask your opinion on the continued uptick in violence against your fellow authors," I stated matter of factly. The way his smirk disappeared immediately I could see he wasn't expecting the Q&A to go down this path. "What situations, if any, do you believe your lack of support has influenced?" I kept my tone very neutral and professional, although I was dying a bit inside. I really wanted to lash out and tell him exactly what I thought of him.

"I... uh... I don't understand the question." He mumbled.

"Excuse me, could you repeat that?" I had heard

him perfectly fine, but I planned to make him uncomfortable, and it appeared I was succeeding.

"I guess what I'm trying to say is, I don't understand why you're asking me that. I don't believe I have done anything..."

I cut him off. "Exactly, you haven't done a single thing. In fact, you stood by, and with the same group I might add, that provoked the torching of Mile Grove Public Library, resulting in the death of..."

"I wasn't there. I..."

"Oh, but you were, I saw you clear as day in video footage. I recognized the New York Mets hat you're wearing right now." I've never been a baseball fan, to me wearing a Mets hat was akin to sportin' a Members Only jacket but everyone knew Ben by it.

"Listen, I don't know where you are getting your information, but I have always supported my fellow authors. The recent tragedies that have taken place in the community are devastating and my heart goes out to every family affected by this onslaught. I have led my local prayer group in many an invocation for the holy spirit to quell the hearts of those who would do harm. I often post scripture on my social media accounts imploring the necessity of accepting the Lord as your savior." He crossed his arms and sat back as if his weird little religious spiel validated his actions or lack thereof.

"And your clandestine meet-ups with Eve Easterly? A known advocate for the cancel culture."

"Nothing clandestine about it, when someone, anyone, reaches out needing guidance I…"

"At a motel?" I retorted.

He shrugged "Wherever."

"Well while you're out there doing 'God's work,' your fellow authors and who you call friends, are being marked! Hell, one of them had their dick melted right off!"

"For the last time, it was hot sauce!" A voice yelled from the back of the room. "There is nothing wrong with little Gage, I mean he's not little… you get what I mean. He still works perfectly fine." He said while giving the nod to the few females sitting near him. "Anyway…" he gave us a little hand wave to continue.

"Libraries and bookstores are being burned to the ground, these aren't random acts of arson, they are orchestrated targets. And you think this world of ours would be inconceivable without the practical existence of a religious belief?"

"I do, yes. That's a great quote, something I've said before?" he replied with a smug grin.

"No, that was Hitler."

"Excuse me," he said with a meek chuckle "you learn something every day."

"You still haven't answered my question. What is your stance on what is going on in the indie horror community?"

"I stand with my brothers and sisters in their right to

creative freedom, no one should be condemned over how they choose to express their art, regardless of subject matter."

"So, you don't agree with the actions taken against them?"

"Absolutely not!"

"But you remain quiet and tethered to the voice of the cancel movement?"

"I'm not tethered to anyone."

"So you're just fucking them?"

"Yes... I mean, no. I mean, I understand why some people feel that horror is ..." He was stuttering to find purchase in his defense.

"You understand? So, you're sympathetic to their movement?"

"Yes."

"Yes?"

"I mean no. No."

"Well, which is it? Either you do or you don't. You can't be on both sides. Nobody likes a Nazi Jew Ben."

He sat there motionless, never breaking eye contact with me for what felt like minutes. The humid, stagnant air in the room was thick with contempt from both sides. The corner of his mouth lifted in an unsettling smirk, "Opinions can be such a heavy burden to shoulder, words carry weight, you'd do yourself a favor in remembering that."

BOOM... BOOM... BOOM...

Suddenly three explosions rocked the room. Everyone froze as we were inundated with ceiling debris raining down on us from above. The only movement I detected was Deven pulling me down and covering my body with his own.

"Wha... what just happened? Was that an earthquake?" I heard a frightened voice about 20 yards away ask.

"Sounded like cannon fire." Came from another voice.

"Maybe someone crashed their car into the building?" Someone else suggested.

"Naw, that ain't sound like no car wreck I ever heard." A voice interjected from across the room.

"Is everyone okay?" Someone asked.

Deven and I stood up and checked each other over, brushing off the layer of dust from our hair and clothes. A shrieking scream broke through the crowd's affirmative responses, and we all turned in its direction. I couldn't see what the woman was looking at on the floor behind the row of chairs but the look in her eyes sent chills up my spine. I felt the spray from the sprinklers before I heard the assault of alarms blasting through the building, a small tremble was felt throughout as the structure settled.

"We need to get the hell out of here." Someone shouted.

The muffled sounds of chaos could barely be heard over the bellow of the fire alarm.

BOOM... BOOM...

Two more explosions came back-to-back. This time nobody froze, panic immediately ensued, and we all rushed to the doors. Fragments of the plaster pelted down, slowing no one in their frenetic intent to escape. I only caught a glimpse as Deven rushed me past the source of the scream minutes earlier, she lay in a pool of blood, her skull crushed by a piece of the ceiling. She was gone but what lay in front of us was so much worse than any horror story I had ever read.

I couldn't see where we were going, the smoke was acting like a black shroud, covering what would become a mass grave. Trying to cover my face from the mixture of drywall, ash, and water that had created a tar-like substance that ran into my eyes proved futile. My vision blurred, my eyes stung, and the fear of losing my only anchor increased with every terrified person that barreled into us. My foot caught on an object and before I could rectify my step, I felt his hand, moist from sweat, lose its grip as I fell through the abyss to the ground below.

The air was colder down here, and my brain could not reconcile how that could be in only a matter of feet. I reached to unhook my foot from its snare. The spongy wet object in my hand made no sense to me, what could I have tripped on? It wasn't until I saw the blood, did I realize it was flesh, a person, or something that used to be attached to one. The leg had no owner yet was still warm from the memory of it.

"Deven!" I screamed. I could taste the death on my tongue, and feel the scorch invade my lungs like fog rolling in. Where was he? Had he just kept going? Didn't he realize I was no longer in the safety of his grasp? "Deven... where are you?" I cried out again, "Please... I don't know where to go." I stood, trying to gather my bearings, my sense of direction unable to guide me. Suddenly relief washed over me as two hands firmly grabbed my shoulders. I spun around, expecting to look into the eyes of protection. What stood in front of me was no longer human but an amalgamation of agony, blood pouring from the dozens of nails embedded in their tissue.

The sound escaping from my mouth wasn't a scream, but a plea, a desperate cry to wake up from this nightmare.

"Hep...eee," it moaned, "Hep...mmm..."

"I'm sorry, God, I'm so sorry. Please... please let me go... I can't... I don't know what to do...I..." I sobbed, trying to break free. I closed my eyes tight. *This can't be real, this can't be real, please God, someone help me,* I silently begged.

"Let her go!"

"Deven!" I sobbed, the tears finally breaking free from my eyes as he wrenched me out of the dying man's clutch. I clung to him, "I called for you... I fell... I didn't know where..."

"Shhh... you're okay, I'm here... shhh." He pulled me tighter into him. "Listen, we have to move, okay?"

"No, what if we get separated again? What if..."

He took my face in his hands, "I will not let you go."

"But what if I..."

"I know you're scared... I'm scared too, but I am not going to let anything happen to you. Look at me... look at me, I need you to hear my voice. This place is on fire, it is rapidly filling with smoke, soon we will not be able to breathe."

I nodded, "Okay."

"Okay... whew... okay," he said, giving me a small smile. "Hold tight to my arm and as much as you'll want to close your eyes, I need you to focus, just look straight ahead and keep moving."

"Okay."

He was right, I didn't want to see any of this.

As we traversed this landscape of broken, lifeless bodies and pools of blood that formed around the amputated limbs, the fire spread rapidly behind us like a sick game of tag. The people it caught roared in agony and writhed on the floor in a desperate attempt to save the skin that was liquifying off their bones. Others were frantically pulling the nails that had lodged in their flesh out, viscous fluid poured from these wounds, unable to be stopped as there were just too many wounds to put pressure on at once.

We made it to the ballroom doors that were no longer there, replaced by a cavernous black void of swirling smoke. We were met with silence as we hastily passed by. What had once housed over eighty tables, was now a graveyard of smoldering books and their makers. A lonely, scorched banner waved from a pillar in the entryway, encouraging guests to stop by Mike Salt's table and grab a copy of his new book, This All Ends Horribly. The irony was not lost on me. My stomach clenched as the sudden realization hit me that most, if not everyone in that ballroom at the time the bombs went off, probably didn't make it out.

The cacophony of cries of anguish and sheer panic assaulted us as we came around the corner to a horde of people trying to escape through the lobby's entrance. Slipping on the gore-covered marble, clamoring for absolution from the torment, it was hard to tell who of them were still amongst the living. *"Through me, you go into a city of weeping; through me, you go into eternal pain; through me, you go amongst the lost people,"* I whispered to myself.

"What?" Deven looked over at me quizzically.

I just shook my head and replied, "Dante's Inferno."

He pulled me in tighter as the glass lobby doors shattered. "Stay close to me" he said, foraying into the bedlam. I closed my eyes when the cool breeze touched my face, for a moment it almost felt like a dream, like when I opened them, I'd see Deven calmly sleeping next to me, his exhalation causing a soft whistle.

Firefighters rushed past us into the building, shouting commands to one another. Paramedics were in a state of distress, unable to attend to all the injured at once. Police officers were fraught with trying to keep everyone calm and organized. My senses were so over-stimulated in the midst of all the havoc, I did not see the assembled mass of radicals initially, a swarm of cancel culture supporters had descended on this tragedy. Shouts of triumph and vindication echoing over the roar of the dying, those trying to escape the miasma were met with violence; accusations of devil worship, pedophilia, baby killing, misogyny, and every other vile act of immorality being hurled at them. They had barely made it out with their lives, only to have to fight for it again. Human walls were forming like a revolting set up of Red Rover, there was no way through, they brought the fight to our doorstep, and we were unarmed.

Law enforcement was ill-prepared to handle this ambush, no one could have predicted the inhumanity that would ensue following such a merciless act of genocide. The death toll climbed. Those who were too weak to defend themselves fell at the hands of their attackers. Deven navigated us through the throng, fighting off the ones attempting to cause us harm as best he could. I felt arms wrap around my waist lifting me off the ground, the only visible attribute of my assailant was a Celtic cross tattooed on his wrist, an image that would wake me up, covered in sweat, unable to catch my breath for years to come.

"Deven!" I screamed "Deven!" He turned to see me struggling to break free, reaching for him as I was being carted off. I watched as he threw his attacker off him and lunged for me, I felt his fingers intertwine with mine and seize a hold, the look in his eyes instantly changed from reassurance to terror as his grip relaxed. "Deven?" He maintained eye contact as his body slumped to the ground. The man he had thrown off moments ago, was now standing over him, bloody knife in hand.

"NOOOOO!!!" I shrieked, "Let me go! Let me go!... DEVEN!" I thrashed with everything I had until my captor finally gave up and relinquished his hold. I fell to the road and crawled to where Deven lay, his breathing labored, I took his head in my lap. "HELP! Someone please help us!" I begged. My plea was lost in the deafening battle going on around us.

Tears continued to zig-zag down my soot-covered face long after the life left Deven's eyes, his upper body safely in my arms as I rocked back and forth quietly praying for the help that would never come.

WEEK EIGHT

Duncan Ralston Officially Declared Dead

Local law enforcement responded to a call sometime last week... yada, yada.

Road crews had reported coming across a suspicious bag on their route...

The plastic trash bag contained articles of clothing, drenched in what appeared to be blood...

Called it in...

I kept scanning the article, why had he been declared dead? Doesn't that take years without a body? What had they found?

Cadaver Dogs searched the area... yeah, yeah.

Evidence found near a cliff approximately one hundred yards from the location of a discarded bag led authorities to believe he had gone over the side...

Search crews came up empty handed after several days...

Traces of urine and blood from an unknown male found at scene...

"What the fuck! So, he was murdered?" I exclaimed.

Samples collected from the multiple articles recovered from inside the bag were sent out for immediate analysis...

Shit... shit... shit...

DNA testing confirmed. Blood specimens were a match to Duncan R. Ralston.

The statement had been released the morning of the convention. However, I had not seen it until a few days later. I had decided to stay with my parents for a while after being released from the hospital with only minor cuts and bruising. I wasn't ready to face the emptiness of my apartment, so my dad went to pick up a few things for me, including my laptop. Knowing that the bombing would be the focus, I avoided social media for the first few days. Unfortunately, that didn't quell the anxious, painful rage that burned throughout my soul. Especially when I was watching the news. I learned SlaughterCon was not the only event that had been assailed that day. Multiple attacks were carried out, at signings, book fairs, markets and shows; casualties were in the thousands, with hundreds more in critical condition. Victims were being airlifted to rural hospitals and care facilities in the smaller surrounding towns, as a result of the metro medical centers being overrun. The protesting and rioting had become rampant across the U.S., with several radical groups joining in the foray, fingers pointed at anyone and everyone who writes or supports horror in literature as the bane of society that requires immediate cessation.

I was in no mood to listen to my mom lecture my dad that if she had joined the seminary like her parents wanted her to, she wouldn't have to remind Jesus to take out the trash or clean the gutters. I quietly slipped into the kitchen to snag a bottle of wine from the rack and head up to my old room.

"Hun, that's for special occasions." Damn, she saw

me, hopefully the sermon won't come until after the buzz kicks in.

I held up the bottle as I continued up the stairs, "I'm home to visit my wonderful parents, it is a special occasion."

Flopping onto my bed like I used to do when I was back in high school, was oddly comforting. Thinking about how hard I thought life was being a teenager made me chuckle. Just like back then, I grabbed my laptop to immerse myself in any other world but my own. I crossed my legs, propped the bottle in between them and dove in.

A Kardashian is getting divorced, big surprise.

Taylor Swift concert sold out in minutes.

Grey's Anatomy is celebrating its 329th season.

People Magazine names celebrity author Steven Pajak Sexiest Man Alive.

Really? This is news. I rolled my eyes, what is this world coming to. I took another big swig of mom's celebratory vino and clicked on Duncan's Facebook page.

Over the last few days everyone had been posting their condolences, memories and photos upon hearing he had been declared dead:

Duncan was a good friend but a mediocre writer.
My thoughts and prayers go out to his friend and cactus. Even as I type this, I'm still in shock. The world will forever be deprived of potential literary

classics like WOOM 2: Inside Man, Puzzle House: The Missing Piece, and Diddy Island Bloodbath. Duncan, my neighbor from the north, may you roam the grounds of Ghostland, intimidating the living with your perpetual get-off-my-lawn scowl.
—Nick Roberts, author of the book that beat Duncan in the Indie Author Brawl

I have never actually read one of Nick's publications, but I hear he writes books for the kind of people that need warning labels on everything. Explains why he's so popular...

No one wants to be in a position where they have to write an obituary for a friend. It feels like writing a blurb for the tome of success that is Patrick C. Harrison III, Paul Giamatti, Duncan Ralston's (?) life and writing career. Cut so short... just like him. Maybe that was a grand joke of the universe, let him only live a decade per foot in height... I'm getting off topic. Duncan was a incredibly versatile author with a sharpness to his storytelling that was unmatched. His books varied from the over-the-top extreme to the intense and elevated character piece. He was always smiling... if you looked at him upside down. I think that was a Canadian thing. Now that Dunkie is gone, there is a tiny, miniscule really, void in the horror

community that simply cannot be filled. Until we see you again in that Lonely Motel in the sky, we will save woom in our hearts for little Dunkaroo.
—Megan Stockton

I can't believe Duncan is dead. We just signed the contract for Try Not to Die: By Autoerotic Asphyxiation. He promised he'd be safe. But no, he couldn't keep those dirty little hands off himself and now he's just another author who failed hard at trying not to die.
—Mark Tullius

Duncan was... well a lot of things. He was Canadian, that's one thing. He was pretty grumpy sometimes, so that's two things Duncan was. Two things...hmm... he liked movies, which, you know, who doesn't amiright? That counts as a thing, right? I'm counting it as a thing. But when you get right down to it, Duncan was a kind man. A good man. At the heart of it, Duncan was my friend and he always made me smile. RIP Duncan Ralston, writer of words. You will be missed.
—Angel Van Atta

Friends, colleagues and Canadians, a hero among us has died. Understandably it's pretty 50/50 with some being upset and others rejoicing. Cancel

culture runs rampant and Duncan was always being chased. Kiss your career goodbye if you say or write the wrong thing. Horror is a different beast where some edgelords can thrive. I think that's how he survived as long as he did. I'll miss you buddy and make sure I have a spot on that hockey team in the sky, eh.
—Shaun Hupp

Shaun was right, opinions were divided. One thing was for sure though, Duncan had left a lasting impression in the community. I'd bet money some hack takes this opportunity to write about him and his death. People have no shame.

I am devastated to hear the news of Duncan's untimely passing. He was one of the first indie horror authors I read and one of my first friends in the horror community. Duncan always got a bad rap because people couldn't separate the man from the fiction, but he was truly one of the kindest people. I hope some asshole doesn't decide to write a book about him and then have the audacity to ask me to edit it.
—Jyl Glenn

I'm sad to hear about Duncan's passing. I guess I'll never see those ten bucks I lent him. I'd like to call

Duncan a friend, because it makes me sound nicer than when I call him a piece of shit. I'm not bitter that his obituary is outselling all of my books, but I am bitter that a fake Facebook profile called Duncan's Traffic Cones has more followers than I do. Even in death that son of a bitch has to outshine me.
—Gage Greenwood

I hate to hear about losing Duncan Ralston. He was a great voice within the horror community. As my mom's favorite horror author, Duncan will be missed by her more than me. Now with him passing on, maybe she'll like my books better. Thoughts and prayers to the Ralston family.
—Jay Bower

Jay Bower... Jay Bower... I repeated the name in my head, it sounded familiar, I had to look up what he had written. Real name: Jaymall Bowerhausen. Shiiit, no wonder he shortened it. That's a mouthful, even if I wasn't half a bottle in.

Duncan truly brought joy to the lives of those around him. He taught us all so many things in his short time here, including teaching us all how to speak Canook, showing us the benefits of maple syrup, and proving to us that Canada is a real

place. Without him, the significance of a shady motel and the traffic cone would be lost upon the world. I'm going to miss his crappy movie suggestions clogging my Facebook feed; now I'll never know what films to avoid. Duncan's footprint on this earth will honestly last a relatively short time because of erosion and crappy Canadian winters will erase it. But he will be missed.
—Heather Ann Larson

I was sad to hear about the passing of Duncan Ralston. He was a dear friend and I'll probably miss him. I remember him telling me how my book 10 Drink Minimum (which is available on Amazon or by messaging me directly) inspired him to keep writing. I remember when I was writing Candy Dish (also available on Amazon or by directly messaging me), Duncan would say 'Matt, there is King, Lovecraft, Barker and then you, who stands above them all.' I will miss his unwavering faith in me. So, in his honor, I'll be putting both my books on sale, and joining my Patreon will be discounted. It's what he would have wanted. Rest in power.
—Matt Lutton

Oh, get the fuck outta here with this guy. I briefly clicked on his profile, "What is your story Mr. Lutton..."

Batman... paints action figures... "Yep, this guy lives in his mom's basement." Big Nickelback fan... single... "Shocker." I said with a chuckle and popped back over to Duncan's to continue reading.

Waking up to hear the news of Duncan's passing came as a shock at first, then I remembered his terrible takes on movies, his eerie love of Catfish nuggets, and unyielding stance on whether or not traffic cones were for external use only. I guess I'm not surprised at all. It was just all too much for our little maple leaf. Fly high Duncster! The potatoes can't get you now.
—RJ Roles

RIP Duncan. It's sad to see someone go that I only knew that he knew I existed when I was a line in a rap song of his, or he comments on my Nicholas Cage posts. You were truly a Canadian. Rot in hell.
—Mike Salt

Fuuuck, Mike must have posted this before the attack. My mom had told me she saw on the news, they initially thought he'd been killed when the three bombs in the ballroom went off, but his body ended up being recovered from a dumpster behind the hotel. It appeared he had crawled inside to hide but ended up getting trapped when a heavy piece of the roof landed on it. He was found two days later.

Someone posted the link to the memorial the hotel was hosting today in honor of those who had lost their lives. The event page had photos of all the victims, three hundred and seventy-two. I scrolled until I found his. Deven's eyes stared back at me from the picture, I didn't know when it was taken but he looked happy, he was always happy. Unlike me who disappeared into a bottle when shit went south, he took the negative with grace and moved forward. I just sat here and looked at him for a while, letting the memory of the last several months come to the surface. "I'm sorry." I spoke to the picture and took another big swig of wine, wiping the trickle from the corner of my mouth and the tears that had gathered at the corners of my eyes.

"God Dammit." I jumped off the bed, tipping over the rest of the wine. Still in my sweats and the oversized Ozzy t-shirt I'd slept in, I slipped on my shoes and jogged down the stairs.

"Where do you think you're going, young lady?" My mom said from the couch.

"The memorial." I replied as I grabbed my purse and my parents' keys to the car.

"I thought you didn't want to attend, how much have you had to drink? You shouldn't be driving. Why don't you just come sit down, sweetie? We'll watch some tv and forget about this sad business." She suggested as she stood to come towards me.

I spun on my heels to face her, "Stop! I don't want to forget. Ever."

I left my mom standing in the entryway and slammed the door behind me.

There was a temporary fence surrounding the front of the hotel, clean up and reconstruction had begun. They had set up a podium on a small makeshift stage for anyone who wanted to say a few words. People had covered the rungs of the fence in flowers, cards, stuffed animals and pictures of their loved ones who'd perished. I kept my distance; I didn't want anyone to recognize me as having been there that day. The news crews who were covering the memorial were within earshot and I could hear them relaying the events of the bombing into their microphones.

"As you can see behind me, this is quite a turn out. Friends, family and fans of the deceased have gathered to pay their respects. Several have taken the stage to share memories or give a tribute to a life gone too soon." The reporter said. *"Many have stated their shock and disappointment that Matt Shaw is not in attendance today, it was reported to us earlier that he had been a featured guest expected to appear at this convention last week but*

had to pull out at the last minute, leaving many to specu-late on his involvement. Despite ongoing efforts, Matt Shaw could not be reached for comment." I rolled my eyes, *leave the poor guy alone already*, I thought. *He just lost his friend, he's probably grieving.*

I slowly made my way a bit closer to the crowd but stopped suddenly when I saw Mrs. Vankirk step up to the podium. She looked out over the crowd, tears welled in her eyes as she gave a small heartbroken smile to the onlookers. "My son was an only child…" she began.

I felt my legs give out, the weight of it all forcing me to my knees, because sometimes it hurts, it hurts so much you feel like your chest is caving in. And the only thing stopping it are the gasps of air you take in between the tears.

WEEK NINE

Interview with Jim Ody, author of Little Miss Evil and Little Miss Evil 2, The Last Weekend, Mystery Island and The Place That Never Existed.

"Hello Jim, thank you for being willing to be a guest

author here on The Best Little Horror House in Texas Podcast with me, your host, Polly Darton."

"I appreciate you having me on."

"I apologize about the early morning; I promise not to keep you too long. For those of you just tuning in, today's guest is Jim Ody, all the way from the UK. Are you ready to get started Jim?"

"Yes ma'am, whenever you're ready."

"So, Jim, what made you choose horror as your preferred genre to write in?"

"As a teenager my true passion was romance. When my friends were sneaking nudie mags from the shelves of convenience stores, I was swiping Cartland, Cooper and Collins, like they were my Hefner, Flint and Guccione. I held an interest in wonders of throbbing members and juicy gussets, where two souls come together in a frantic passionate climax – all wrapped up in a package of fantasy."

"That's very, ahem, interesting. I never would have guessed you would be a lit-erotica fan"

"It was my dirty little secret, and to conform, I added violence and bloodshed to satiate the tastes of the more depraved. I wasn't part of this. I didn't want it. But horror wanted me; and I was a literary whore down on my luck and tickling keys for whatever money came my way. And now I'm known for blood splattering flesh, rather than rivers of love dripping down satisfied thighs."

chuckle "That's um, descriptive. I can understand now why you incorporate intimate scenes into your books. Gearing the stories to your fans but tossing in a little bit of you in there too. I'm curious if other authors do that as well."

"I wouldn't know."

"Do the accusations that have been thrown at horror authors deter you at all from continuing to write in this genre?"

"I've blurred the lines between romance and horror, bathing in the obscene and washing off any purity I ever had. The mask of envy has many shades and ignorance will always attract hate. Love and lust, pain and suffering, I narrate the lives of those who wish to feel, not be numb with the mundane. If that's wrong, then let the Devil judge me."

"Intriguing way to look at it, especially when the cancel culture is running rampant. Do you feel you've been affected personally by it? Or has the UK in general faced the same backlash as here in the states for example?"

"The pressures from all around can either make or break you. I've always been a loose cannon. A keyboard maverick who types whilst wearing two pairs of underwear for protection. For it to affect me, would be for me to say I had control of my life and what I write. I don't. The Devil wakes me up with flaming hot breath, and I am nothing more than his bitch as words ejaculate onto

virgin white pages. That being said, I've bought more underwear. I may need to start wearing three pairs."

chuckling "Probably not a bad idea considering present circumstances, many authors and others in the indie industry have even expressed their hesitation to leave the house these days after so many lives have already been lost. What do you think of all the attacks on your fellow colleagues?"

*"Art is expressive, and sadness only engulfs those who don't fully understand death. It's not the end, anyone who's seen the movie Trick or Treat knows that! Shit, Ozzy was in it for God's sake!" *Jim sighs* "I mean, pancake sales would drop without Lutton. And Mike Salt's unfortunate passing, knowing there won't be any more of his videos, tugs at the heart strings... but some of the others... it was inevitable. Some people are just too much. I'm surprised I've lasted this long. Should I feel regret? Worry? I don't know. People are fucking crazy, that's all I know."*

"You look a bit apprehensive, maybe a little afraid?"

Jim shrugs and wipes a tear that was forming at the corner of his eye

"Alright. Let's move on. It shook the indie community when Duncan Ralston went missing, no doubt the catalyst to where we are now as a society. As I'm sure you've heard, he was recently declared deceased. What was your reaction upon hearing the news?"

"I was surprised. I just assumed he'd been 'missing' much longer. The AI persona that has been brandished around like some Weekend at Bernie's reject was laughable. Ralston has always been into some shady underground shit. He's a legend, makes me look like some bloody Snow White. Am I shocked at the backlash? Of course not. This is millennial panic, and I bet you somewhere Ralston is pulling the strings, laughing his arse off! Is he dead?... Listen, Duncan Ralston is bigger than all of us. Mark my words... nothing is what it seems."

"That's a pretty lofty theory Jim. Any evidence to back it up?"

"Call it a hunch"

"Well in that case, what about Matt Shaw? No one seems to be able to get in touch with him either."

"Matt Shaw... that guy is a survivalist. You could pick him up, drop him on an uninhabited island and within twelve months that place would be thriving with smiling, happy people... and probably goats. There would be a whole village built up, like huts, and a full-on cult like atmosphere. I'm not saying a David Koresh type necessarily, but he'd sport a look that merged Russell Brand and Jesus, with a compendium of their ideologues and symbolism. Basically, what I'm saying here is, think about it. The answers are there... if you're willing to look. Shaw will only show himself, if he wants you to see him..."

"Whew, it's about time to wrap up, you've given us

all a lot to think about Jim. We want to thank you again for joining us on the podcast, it's definitely been interesting. And we wish you the best in all your future projects."

"Thanks for having me."

"Alright listeners, that was Jim Ody, thank you all for tuning in. Please join us next week where we will be reading through and discussing our favorite, funniest one-star reviews."

I stood to leave. It was a bad idea coming here, my mom was right; I'm too emotional and too intoxicated. Mrs. Vankirk was still at the podium, but I was willfully tuning her out, I hadn't known Deven all that long. The way she spoke made me feel as if I'd known him my whole life, at least that's how the pain of his memory felt.

I started back to the car when out of the corner of my eye I caught Eve Easterly breaking away from the crowd. *What the fuck is she doing here?* She turned and started walking in the opposite direction I was going but blind rage took over and I decided to follow. I sped up my pace so I could get closer, we were now a block away from the memorial. I maintained my fifty-yard distance, not that she would necessarily know who I was if she did see me. Up ahead a man exited a parked vehicle from the passenger side and started walking toward her. I couldn't see his face, but I recognized the ballcap. *Ben Young, that son of a bitch, I knew it!!*

He wrapped his arms around her waist and leaned down to give her a small kiss. *Motherfucker!* They turned and walked towards the car, Ben getting into the passenger side while Eve slid into the driver's seat.

I didn't remember grabbing the pipe, or even where I got it from, but the next thing I knew, I was screaming at the top of my lungs with every **WHACK** against her windshield. "THIS... IS... FOR... DEVEN!" **WHACK** "THIS... IS... FOR... EVERYTHING... YOU... TOOK... FROM... ME!" **WHACK** "THIS... IS... FOR... ALL... THE... DEATHS... YOUR... ACTIONS... CAUSED!" I was running out of breath, but I hoisted it over my head again and again.

"WHOA, WHOA, WHOA!" Ben shouted getting out of the car. "What the fuck is your problem, lady?" He was yelling, as he came around the car towards me.

"What the fuck is my problem?! You're killing my friends is my fucking problem." I said, stepping towards him, the pipe still firmly locked in my grip.

He put up his hands, "Hey, I don't know who you think we are, but we had nothing to do with hurting your friends... Wait! Aren't you the crazy bitch from the panel the other day? The one that was yelling at me. Eve!... Eve! Look, it's the chic I told you about, the one who thinks I killed that librarian."

"I've called the police." Eve stated as she stood up

out of the car. "You'll pay for fucking up my car." She said, glaring at me.

"Just put the pipe thing down and we'll let the police sort it all out. They'll tell you, I'm not responsible for whatever delusions you're having."

"Delusions! Delusions!" I took several steps towards him as he took several steps back. "Was E.L. Giles a delusion? What about Mile Grove Library? And Deven? Was he a fucking delusion too?!! Was cradling him as he died in my arms all just in my head you self-righteous prick?!"

"What? You think I'm just traveling all over the country offing people and making it look like an accident? What is more likely? That or you are needing a medication adjustment because you're clearly a goddamned nut job."

"The cops are several minutes out, there's no one currently available to come help." Eve called over to Ben, phone still pressed against her ear. "Yeah, I said she has a fucking weapon, she bashed my window in... well, could you hurry it up, this bitch is unhinged."

I looked back and forth between the two of them. Eve half in and half out of her car, Ben on the sidewalk, hands still part way up. What was my plan here? I looked down at my hands, knuckles white from squeezing so hard and started to lower the pipe.

"Ben! Grab it from her, you idiot!" Eve cried out. He lunged for it and missed.

"No!" I raised it up again. "You do not get to play this game anymore!" I yelled as I walked towards him. "You may not have personally killed these people, but you knew, you knew, and you did nothing!" He was backing up away from me and I followed him, continuing to make sure he heard every word I had to say. "You side with people who would ruin others to make themselves seen; you criticize the cancel cult but then fuck them later that night." He took a step forward and I swung.

"Whoa, okay, calm down." He retreated again.

"Calm down?" ***SWING*** "Calm down?" ***SWING*** "I'm perfectly calm, I've never been so fucking calm!" ***SWING***

"You've made your point okay. You're not going to do anything, or you would have already. You're pissed, I get it. You lost your friend, boyfriend, whatever but doing something stupid isn't going to bring him back. I wrote a story once that..." And he was gone.

I was so blind with rage I had not seen the orange cones and caution tape behind him, but I did hear the sickening crunch when he hit the bottom of the manhole and the blood curdling "Ben!!!" Eve released.

"Help!" Eve pleaded on her knees beside the hole "Somebody help! Ben? Ben, can you hear me?" She called out over and over.

I dropped the pipe, turned, and calmly walked away.

INTERLUDE

"What the fuck was that?" I exclaimed, glancing into the rearview mirror, afraid to take my eyes off the road in front of me in case there was anything else. The sudden loud *thunk...thunk...thunk* and a hard jerk to the right abruptly informed me of a flat.

"It appears whatever it was fucked your tire, mate."

"And they say you're an imbecile."

"Who says that?!" Matt shot back.

"Oh everyone... yeah that Matt Shaw guy, he'd be out of his depth in a mud puddle. Musta snuck into the gene pool when the lifeguard wasn't looking." I said while glancing at him and winking.

Well shit, I thought. I hope the spare is in decent shape; I went to exit the car to go inspect it.

"Do you want to hear a joke?" Matt asked.

"Are you serious? We're stuck on the side of the road in the middle of nowhere, and you want to tell a joke? Okay fine, what's your joke?" I groaned, but humored him anyway.

"Good," he said as he sat up straighter. "What is the difference between a vitamin and a hormone?"

I stared back at him with a blank expression.

"Come on! What is the difference between a vitamin and a hormone?"

"Shit, I don't know, what is the difference?"

"You can't make a vitamin..." he replied, the corners of his mouth curling up, not unlike the grinch.

"Jesus Christ, dude." I said, shaking my head and chuckling. "Now, are you going to get off your ass and help me change this tire?"

"Nah, mate, that's all you."

"Gee, thanks," I said, rolling my eyes. "At least get out of the car, so I can jack this thing up."

A few minutes later I had the spare ready, the car lifted, and three out of the five lug nuts removed, the fourth giving me some trouble. "Hey, could you come help me with this, it ain't budging."

We both wrenched on that thing until we were out of breath, without success.

"Here, let's try this." Matt said, holding up a softball sized rock.

"What are you planning on doing with that?"

"I don't know, hitting it, I guess." He replied with a shrug.

He beat on the lug wrench to no avail. I crouched to get a better look when I was struck in the head by something flying off the wheel well.

"I got it loose!" Matt exclaimed triumphantly. "Oh, shit, mate, you're fucking bleeding! What the fuck happened?"

"The damn rock you were bashing the wrench fucking thing with bounced off and hit me." I replied holding my hand to my forehead to stop the bleeding, but I could see it had already soaked my shirt.

Matt reached through the window into the car and grabbed a bottle of water, "Here, rinse it off, let's see how bad it is."

I poured the water over my head and then splashed it on my face to rinse the blood off.

"Tis but a scratch." he jested.

"Funny," I replied. "Well, my shirt is ruined and probably my shorts. There's a first aid kit under the front seat of the driver's side. And will you grab my bag out of the trunk so I can change?"

"Sure, sure, head wounds bleed like mad, but they're usually not as serious as they first look. Serves you though for taking the piss out of me earlier."

"I don't even know what that means." I said as I started to pull off my blood-soaked clothes.

"It means... you know what, forget it. Here's your duffle, the kit, and a plastic bag to put the clothes in." He said, handing me everything. "Bollocks! I've got to change the bloody tire now, don't I?"

Listening to Shaw's grumbling and cursing while I attempted to bandage the gash on my forehead lifted my mood and gave me a great idea for a story about two idiots getting stuck in the middle of nowhere, encountering all sorts of terrifying comedic scenarios. He was right though; the cut wasn't bad.

I tossed my stuff back into the trunk and bagged up the bloody clothes, deciding just to toss them in the trash the next time we stopped. Looking around I didn't see Shaw anywhere, *now where the hell did he get off to?* "Matt!" I hollered out. "Dude where'd you go?" I heard a muffled shout come from the woods; I couldn't tell what he said but I headed in that direction.

"Why'd you wander off?" I asked when I found him. "It's going to get dark soon, we should probably get back on the road."

"Went to take a piss and heard water, thought it

might be a creek or something, I wanted to check it out."

"Yeah, we should be close to the river along here."

"It's over the cliff" nodding his head.

I took a few steps forward and peered over the side, "Whew, that's a fucking drop." The head wound made my vertigo intensify.

"You're getting close to that edge, mate. Thinking about jumping?"

"Maybe," I smirked back at him.

"Get your arse back." He grabbed hold of my arm. "You go over that edge and they'll think I offed you."

"Ya never know, being accused of murder might boost your sales."

"Sod off." He said as he turned and started heading back toward the car.

"Shit!" I said out loud after we had been back on the road for over thirty minutes. "We gotta turn around."

"What the fuck for?"

"I left the bag of my bloody clothes on the side of the road."

WEEK ELEVEN

Nick had been waiting all day for this. He poured the last five-gallon bucket of ice into the rinsed-out yard-waste bin and grabbed the hose to fill it. He preferred to do this in the early morning hours but his schedule as of late had not permitted the extra energy it would take to wake up early. The pressures of grading the final assignments before the end of the school year   and barely meeting the deadline to turn in his latest novel had worn him thin. He had become insufferable, according to his wife and she had taken the kids to her sister's for a few days to give him some "privacy to pull his head outta his ass" in her words.

He went into the house to grab the step stool while the bin was filling. He had an overwhelming craving for a beer, a sensation he hadn't had in years. *Maybe I do need to pull my head out of my ass,* he thought as he reached for a can of Alani. He debated about grabbing a towel for after his ice bath, but changed his mind as the weather lately had been unusually warm in the evenings. As he headed back outside,the sound of the doorbell sent a cringe up his spine. "Are you kidding me? I really need to disconnect that fucking thing," he muttered as he headed to answer the door to see who was interrupting his evening.

"Can I help you?" Nick said with clear irritation in his voice. In front of him stood a younger guy in slacks and a white button up shirt and tie, a Latter-Day Saints pin secured to the pocket. *Shit*, Nick cursed in his head.

"Good evening, sir!" He said with a big grin. "I'm from the Church of Jesus Christ of Latter Day Saints, I'm Elder Durgin."

Nick noticed the young man was doing his best to stand straight and appear tall and confident. Nick was still taller and couldn't resist the urge to stand straighter himself to show that fact. "Hey bud, I don't mean to be rude, but I am kind of in the middle of something…"

"Oh, I do apologize for interrupting, this will only take a minute. I am out today visiting neighbors to spread a message of hope…"

Nick cut him off. "Listen kid, I appreciate what you're doing and your commitment to your belief but like I said, I'm in the middle of something. Have a good rest of your night." He shut the door and headed toward the backyard when the doorbell sounded again.

"My apologies for keeping you, but I would like to share a bit of scripture, it will only take a moment. I'm sure whatever you are doing can wait just a bit longer to hear the word of God." He said with a condescending air, Nick almost felt like he was being challenged.

"I said no thank you, kid. But hey listen, do you see that house over there?" Nick pointed across the street and a few houses down to Felix's place. Nick never liked that crotchety bastard who was always chastising the neighborhood kids for getting too close to his prize roses. "I'm pretty sure that guy worships the devil, go talk to him." The kid turned to look and Nick shut the door, chuckling to himself as he hurried out back, and got there just in time to turn the hose off before it overflowed the bin.

The bell went off again just as Nick was unfolding the stool. *What is wrong with this fucking kid?!* Nick angrily thought as he stomped back through the house, readying himself to give this shit a piece of his mind.

"You need to get off my property, I've asked you nicely but you're going too far, I'm going to call your..." Nick started to shout.

"You're not going to do anything but listen, Nick." The kid said calmly.

"How do you know who..."

"Everyone knows who you are, Nick Roberts." he stated, as he loosened his tie and unbuttoned the top few buttons of his shirt. "Guess I won't be needing this either." He tossed aside the Latter Day Saints pin and gave Nick a smirk.

"Who are you and what the fuck do you want?"

"A message."

"Excuse me?"

"A message." he repeated.

"I don't have time for this, get off my property." Nick went to slam the door in his face, but he wasn't fast enough. The kid shot his arm out and held it steadfast.

"What comes out of a person is what defiles them. For it is from within, out of a person's heart, that evil thoughts come. This evil comes from inside them. The wage of sin is death." He admonished, never breaking eye contact but removing his hand from the door. "Do you fall short of the glory of God, Nick?" and with that he turned and walked away.

Nick immediately closed and locked the door, including the chain. He leaned his back against it and let his heart return to a normal rhythm. "Okay, that was officially the weirdest shit that's ever happened to me," he said out loud to no one. He slowly walked to his backyard, unsure if he was still in the mood for his ice bath. That encounter had creeped him out; he had been following the news since everything had started with Duncan's disappearance and the escalation of the attacks on authors, but he had never considered being a target himself.

He had lost a lot of colleagues lately and to say his guard hadn't been up would be untrue. *But coming to my home?* He hadn't heard of that happening. *I guess I should be grateful it was only a religious nut and not one of the radicals.* Breathing a sigh of relief, he decided to get into the ice bath.

He took a deep breath before submerging his body into the below 50-degree water. Closing his eyes he began his meditation to refocus his mind away from the pain. He practically jumped out of his skin when a death metal chord came blasting over the fence from his neighbors' garage. "Jesus Christ!" he gasped. Closing his eyes to attempt to get in the correct mental headspace again proved futile. Between his earlier encounter and teenage Ozzy Osborn next door, this apparently wasn't the night for this. Even though the outside air felt warm on his face, he had read the forecast predicted a cold front coming in and he was feeling hints of it in the breeze now.

He went to stand up and get out when the lid came crashing down on top of his head, forcefully submerging him completely under the icy water. He immediately propelled himself up and was met with resistance and plunged under again. *What the hell was happening?!* The lid was plastic and didn't latch. Did it catch on something? *No, there's nothing it could have caught on.* There was only about four or five inches between the water and the lid, maybe six at its curve. There wasn't enough breathing room for him to be able to fill his lungs and panic started to set in. Without being able to fully contract his diaphragm, he took the biggest breath he could, bent his legs, and pushed with everything he had against the lid. It didn't budge.

Okay, don't panic Nick, he kept repeating. How long had he been in now? Twelve minutes, maybe fifteen. *Just slow your breathing and think.* A noise interrupted his thought. Gravel? He heard the distinct crunch sound the rocks make when being walked on. *Is someone out there? In his backyard?* "Hello?! Is someone out there? Help me please!!" He listened, there it was again, footsteps, but closer this time.

Sixteen minutes. "I'm here! In the yard bin! I'm stuck! The lid won't open." Silence. Was someone out there or was he becoming delirious already? He took another deep breath and plunged under, rocking his body back and forth in the hope of tipping over.

Seventeen minutes. *It's not tipping over, why isn't it tipping over? I can't breathe! No, you can breathe, you're just running out of oxygen. How long has it been now?* "HELP! HELP! Can you hear me?" *Maybe there wasn't anyone out there. Maybe the lack of air is making you hallucinate.*

Eighteen minutes. *Okay, you can do this. Take a deep breath. Squat as low as you can then thrust up. Brace yourself. Rock back and forth. Yeah, that will work. It has to. One... two... three...*

Nineteen minutes. He couldn't hold his breath any longer and sank back down, gasping for what little air was left inside the container. *The phone! Was that the phone ringing inside the house? Yes!* "Amy!! I'm here!! Amy!!" He screamed, knowing she couldn't possibly hear him, but he didn't care. A sudden rush of adrenaline had him punching the lid until his arms gave out and he was choking on mouthfuls of water.

Twenty minutes.He was so cold, or numb, he couldn't tell which. And tired, so tired.

Twenty-one minutes. Had he dozed off? For how long? "Amy... Amy, I'm here." But it only came out as a whisper.

Twenty-two minutes. Darkness invaded him. *Are my*

eyes open? No. Maybe. He couldn't see anything. He couldn't feel anything. *Scraping, I hear scraping.*

The lid.

Gravel.

Footsteps.

Amy...

WEEK TWELVE

"We shall defend our island, whatever the cost may be, we shall fight on the beaches, we shall fight on the landing grounds, we shall fight in the fields and in the streets, we shall fight in the hill; we shall never surrender."

—Winston Churchill

Nick Robert's murder had brought about a maelstrom of epic proportions. Up until the news broke, we had taken a stance of defense over confrontation. No one wanted this, so staying in the shadows had been the unspoken agreement. Stay quiet, keep your head down, and hope the angst and uprising from Cancel Culture would eventually abate. But they killed America's sweetheart. If Duncan was the middle finger of the community, Nick was the apple pie. Both were needed to keep the scale balanced. But, now they're gone and we have nothing left to lose.

Most people will never know what it's like to see their rendering on the evening news. They will never have to sit there, sweating bullets praying to a God they don't believe in, hoping he believes in them. I was a criminal, wanted for the murder of Ben Young. My only saving grace was the sweats I'd worn that day that had made me look much heftier than I was. Thank you, Lululemon. But also fuck you— this is why women have complexes. Luckily, my parents had not put two and two together whenever the sketch of my face was shown on TV. They were far more focused on what everyone had come to call 'The Readkoning,' a hideous amalgamation of 'read' and 'reckoning.' What had started out as a movement to cancel authors whose works people found distasteful or offensive had become a cataclysmic purge of anything and anyone. It was a free-for-all.

If you were brave enough to leave the house, confident you had not pissed off a neighbor— or someone else for that matter who now had it out for you— you were faced with the challenge of finding provisions. Stores were still open-ish, but deliveries were scarce because of trucks being attacked or robbed along their routes. News reports were full of images of all the major U.S. cities on fire, burned-out police cruisers abandoned on the side of what used to be busy streets. On occasion, you'd catch an image of human remains that the stations had not caught in editing. Everyone knew someone who had been killed, but few knew why, and no one seemed able to stop it.

Social media was no longer a place to escape to. Once in a while, a photo of someone proud of the pot roast dinner they'd prepared would pop through, only for them to get torn apart by the masses for posting triviality with all the upheaval taking place around them— as if holding onto whatever happiness you could was a condemnable offense. Most had resorted to chat groups to share information and feel less isolated, but were we friends? No. Blogs, TikToks, and Pages were all but nonexistent; opinions weren't topics open for discussion, they were a death sentence.

It was only by chance I came across a post regarding a memorial for Duncan. I wondered what he would think of his demise ushering in the end of civilization as we knew it. *There he is, the OG of the apocalypse,* I chuckled to myself as I looked at the photo chosen to commemorate him. He was sitting in a lounge chair on vacation, wearing a tank top that says 'Sand Up in This Beach,' holding up some fruity concoction with an umbrella. This whole thing was almost comical, like a poorly written satire by someone who thinks they're funny.

I sat back in my chair to read what Angel had to say.

I hope this request finds everyone as well as they can be in these current circumstances. The state of things weighs heavily on my mind and heart. I have spent many nights deep in thought over what could be done, if anything. I believe going back to where it all began is as good of a place as any to start. Let's choose not to not take the route of anger and accusation, but to come together to celebrate a life instead. Let's do what we should have done in the first place: let's mourn our colleague, the author, the supporter, the nature lover, the traveler, and yes, the edgelord— our friend Duncan Ralston. I have decided to organize a memorial for the week after next to be held at his property. Bring flow-ers, bring books, but above all, bring your happy

memories of the man who pushed our buttons
and our boundaries.
—Angel Van Atta

Shit! When was this posted? Ten days ago, okay. I scrolled down to check the details and figure out a plan to get myself there by next week. I should probably avoid being seen as much as possible; my likeness was still circulating.

I was on the road the next day. After going over the maps and finding indirect routes to avoid the big cities, it was going to take me longer, but I should arrive there the morning of the memorial. It didn't take me long before I started to see the devastation along my way: overturned vehicles, ransacked homes and businesses, and enough caution tape to put the company who made it on the Forbes list. I unfortunately had become indifferent to death—okay, maybe not indifferent, but it no longer crumbled me like it had just three short months ago. But when I came across the animals that had fallen victim to our deplorable behavior, it tugged at me, and I found myself saying a little prayer for their souls, no longer having faith that our species had one.

I stopped for the day in a tiny town I'd never heard of at a cozy motel nestled right off the highway that had been the only one with a vacancy light still shining, or any lights at all for that matter. Most had closed their doors in fear of being the next location of a crime scene. The vending machine offered little in the way of nutrition, so I settled on a bag of Funyuns, Peanut M&M's and a Dr. Pepper. I made myself comfortable in the outdated room. Daylight was still in full force, but I was ready to call it a night. I had left at 4 AM that morning and after ten hours on the road, I was feeling the weight of my undertaking. I turned on the box TV to have some background noise as I took a quick shower, but as I got undressed, I heard the newscaster say they were covering a protest that had turned into a riot of epic proportions.

"I'm coming to you live from Downtown Los Angeles where what started out as a peaceful protest at one of the country's largest independent bookstores, has now become an ebullition of violence. I want to apologize for the shaky feed. I'm having to shoot this from my iphone because the studio's cameras have either been destroyed or stolen over the last several months, so please bear with me."

Wrapped in a towel, I sat at the end of the bed and turned up the volume. I was familiar with that bookstore; they had just reopened last weekend after being closed due to vandalism. The backlash they'd been receiving for the decision to reopen had been appalling; the cancel culture took it as a slap in the face, with the indie community mostly in support but wary after all the attacks.

"An angry crowd has amassed around what looks to be a supporter of the reopening, he's shouting into a bullhorn, but I can't quite make out what he or they are saying. Let me see if I can get a bit closer."

The bouncing around was making me nauseated to watch. *Dude, just stand still and zoom in. There's so much noise; we're not going to be able to make out what they're saying anyway.* I could hear him breathing heavily as he made his way through the horde, but I was only able to catch snippets of surrounding upheaval. 'Burn it down.' 'Jesus hates horror.' 'Freedom of creative speech.' 'Banning books is unconstitutional.' The hate from both sides was evident in the signs' tone. He finally aimed his camera forward toward the mob and zoomed in. *Holy fuck! That's Matt Lutton!!* He stood there, fist raised, talking into the megaphone. All sorts of shit was being thrown at him, but he kept going. *I really wish I could hear what he was saying.*

"Oh fuck! Someone just hit him in the thigh with a baseball bat, just went right up to him and swung... he's down, he's down!! They're surrounding him!!"

Oh my god, someone do something! I could see he was trying to stand up without putting much weight on that leg and back away, but they were inching towards him. *Get closer! Get closer, you idiot!* I yelled at the reporter through the TV. Matt was trying to escape this onslaught, but he was cornered. *Why wasn't anyone helping!!*

"Someone just swung on him! They're still swinging! Shit, there's blood!... Hey!... Hey! Leave him alone! Hey!"

The camera man's demands were completely ignored; he kept shouting for them to back off as he made his way through the crowd. I was only catching glimpses of Matt, but he was hurt; the front of his shirt was becoming soaked in blood. Suddenly, he turned and bolted. *Where did he go? What's going on?* My face was practically pressed against the screen now, and I was rocking back and forth with anxiety. I couldn't see anything!! The guy had obviously dropped the phone down to his side as he followed the procession.

"They're following him, oh God, they're going after him! Hey! Stop! Stop! Shit, shit, shit. What can I do? Hey, you, on the phone! Call the police! There's a man being chased down, he's hurt... they're attacking him... he... bloody shirt...yes, just call... Yes, that building, I'm going...help."

I couldn't catch everything he was saying. I think he had forgotten he was airing this live. All I was seeing was the ground and brief glances of what I thought were his pants. He began to jog, continuing to yell out, trying to stop the attackers. He burst through a door and headed up the stairs. I couldn't tell what kind of building he was in, but I could hear the yells of the angry mob following after Matt. "Get the fuck away from me!" came an echoed distressed shout. "What the fuck is wrong with you? Get away from me!" The camera man's heavy breathing was muffling Matt's cries. *Oh please, please make them stop,* I chanted, still rocking. I couldn't see anything, but I couldn't look away. *Jesus Christ, how many floors was this building?*

"Did you hear that slam? What was that?"

Matt cried out in pain.

"STOP!! You're going to kill him!!"

I could see he'd gone through another door and was now on the roof of the building. *Oh my God, lift your phone up!!* I shouted. I could hear Matt in the background crying out with every hit. Finally, he raised his phone.

· · ·

"Look!! Look!! You all are live!! I'm streaming this entire thing!!" he shouted. Several turned their heads to look at the camera man. "That's right you pieces of shit! Everyone can see what you're doing. Back the fuck away from him!"

Matt was stumbling in the background, hunched over and clutching his abdomen, but still standing. He was beaten and bloody, but he appeared coherent. My heart skipped a beat. *Thank God*, I let out a sigh of relief. The group just stared at the phone pointed at them, a look of confusion on their faces, unsure what move to make next. *Wait, what was that?* The angle made a quick turn to show police officers bolting through the roof's door. The cacophony that erupted made it impossible for me to decipher what was going on.

"They attacked him, I saw the whole thing! I have it right here." I heard the camera man shouting. "Get on the ground... on your knees!" I could hear several voices command, but the phone was bouncing around so much that I wasn't catching much else. It finally steadied, and I could see Matt. He was still staggering, holding his gut, but he was much more alert. He suddenly started laughing hysterically, blood coating his teeth and dribbling down his chin.

"HA! You thought you could kill me?! Look at you!" he chastised them. "Look at what you've become!" He stumbled, but righted himself. "Do you think you accomplished anything? You haven't! I'll heal and come back louder!" His step faltered again, knocking him back.

Oh no! No! No! No! He's going to…

"You can't stop the Batma…………"

"NOOOOOOOO!!"I screamed.

I couldn't get the image of Matt's broken body on the concrete below out of my head. Every time I closed my eyes, I saw his lifeless ones. I saw his skull split open. And the blood pooling beneath him. *Why did the camera guy have to show him going over the edge? Why didn't I look away?*

I didn't leave the motel the next day. I had not slept. Every time I slipped into something reminiscent of sleep, I was visited by a grotesque, fragmented, vision of Matt's corpse and Batman woven together and I would wake up gasping. I didn't even like the guy, but I felt his absence. How can you miss someone you never even knew? Maybe it was the knowledge that now, I never would.

Missing a full day of driving put me behind schedule, so I would have to drive an extra three hours each day to make up for it. I decided to just doze when I needed it at rest stops along the way. I felt less alone on the road than I did in the off-the-beaten-path lodgings. I had ignored news of any kind the first three days back on the road, but I needed to check social media for any updates regarding the memorial. Before I could navigate to Angel's page, my eye caught a response to a random post. The headline read: "DA's office responds to outcry: Will not be filing charges related to ongoing protests." I rolled my eyes, *fuck the DA*. That's not what got my attention. It was a response to the post from three hours ago.

"Has everyone lost their bloody fucking minds!?" Matt Shaw commented.

THE MEMORIAL

"I'm not afraid of Death; I just don't want to be there when it happens."

—Woody Allen

I arrived at 8 AM that morning. According to Angel's instructions, the actual memorial didn't start until noon, but the property was already fanatical with activity. From what I could see, we were unable to park on the property because it was gated at the road, so everyone was parking along the street and hoofing it up his long driveway.

As soon as I stepped out of the car, the noise coming from the gathering in the distance reverberated in my ears. I took a deep breath and headed in the same direction as everyone else. I wanted to be here, but a sinking feeling was building in my stomach. Not just about being recognized, but if recent events were any indication, this wasn't over.

The gathering was larger than I had anticipated when the house and property came into view. At least six or seven dozen people milled about, talking to one another, or standing at the front of the house reading the cards that had been left propped up along his deck amongst hundreds of flower bouquets. I sighed in relief; everyone seemed genuinely happy to be here to give their condolences. I saw Angel weaving her way through the groups, smiling and saying a few words to each before moving on.

I made myself comfortable under a tree several yards from the house. I wasn't in the mood to converse with anyone, so I just closed my eyes and leaned my head back against the trunk and listened. I must have dozed off for a bit because I sat up straight when I heard yelling. Confused, a jolt of panic shot through me when I remembered where I was. I scrambled to my feet to try and get a better look through the crowd to see what was going on.

I was finally able to squeeze myself through enough to see the mob of protesters that had shown up. Angel was in the middle demanding they leave immediately. I could see from the look on her face she was panicking. I couldn't tell what she was saying but her arms were emphasizing whatever point she was trying to make. I kept my eyes on her; however this was going to go, I wanted to follow her lead.

Angel gestured down the driveway, telling the unwelcome guests to get the fuck out. When she accidentally struck one of the protesters, it set off a chain reaction that only escalated by the second. They swung back, knocking Angel to the ground. That was all it took, and we were on them. Three months of torment unleashing at once. I grew up with an older brother so I could take a punch, but over the years I must have softened because it fucking hurt. Ever wonder what an M-80 feels like going off in your nose? Get socked in the face.

I stumbled back after that last hit, this was insane, I couldn't tell who was covered in blood or the red paint the protesters were dousing us with. If this wasn't so fucking pathetic, it would almost be laughable, like someone tried to film a brutal Game of Thrones style battle scene but missed the mark and ended up with Anchorman. There was even a pitchfork laying in the muddy, gory mixture. *Who the fuck brings a pitchfork to a protest? Who'd you think you're confronting? Shrek?*

Angel was trying her damnedest to stop this, running through the crowd pleading "Stop fighting," "You guys are being mean," "You're ruining the grass," "There's a table of refreshments on the deck, I baked cookies, let's just stop all this nonsense," but it was out of control and her pleas went unanswered. I backed away. I loved Duncan, and I would miss the anticipation of his next release, but I wasn't willing to die here. I turned to leave but was forcefully grabbed and spun around.

"Youuuu!" Eve snarled at me, "I was hoping I would see you here."

I was too stunned to move at first. She had a death grip on my collar, and when I went to pull away, I was met with a knife to my throat.

"Did you think it was funny to mock me by wearing a hat like his? Rubbing it in my face that you had gotten away with it? Did you?" She spit in my face. I didn't realize until that moment which of my dad's hats I had grabbed on my way out the door to hide my face, but the humor of the situation wasn't lost on me and I inadvertently chuckled.

"Is this some kind of joke to you bitch?"

"If only Ben was here to explain it to you." I smirked. Every shit I had ever given left when I looked into her eyes. "Do it," I challenged her. I didn't care. Her grip strengthened, and I could feel the fabric of my shirt digging into my neck, cutting off my oxygen. A warm gust hit my face. I averted my gaze away from Eve. I could see Duncan's house ablaze, smoke billowing toward the sky.

The blasting of a horn and the sound of tires on gravel broke through the violence, and as if on cue, everyone stopped mid-swing to turn and look.

As he slowly made his way up the driveway, the filthy and bloodied onlookers parted. He felt like the Wal-Mart version of Moses. He was seeing it, but his brain could not comprehend what was going on. The deer-in-the-headlights expression on everyone's faces was giving him *Invasion of the Body Snatchers* vibes. *What were they all doing here?* He threw the car into park and opened the door to step out. Duncan was met by complete stunned silence and the stare of a hundred shocked faces looking back at him. He scanned the crowd of terrified individuals before his gaze finally landed on his home, completely engulfed in flames.

"What the FUCK, EH!?"

THE END